Sir Arthur Conan Doyle's

THE ADVENTURES OF
SHERLOCK HOLMES

Sir Arthur Conan Doyle's

THE ADVENTURES OF
SHERLOCK HOLMES

BOOK THREE

The Adventure of the Engineer's Thumb
The Adventure of the Beryl Coronet
The Adventure of Silver Blaze
The Adventure of the Musgrave Ritual

Adapted for young readers by
CATHERINE EDWARDS SADLER

Illustrated by ANDREW GLASS

AN AVON CAMELOT BOOK

SIR ARTHUR CONAN DOYLE'S
THE ADVENTURES OF SHERLOCK HOLMES
adapted by Catherine Edwards Sadler
is an original publication of Avon Books.
This work has never before
appeared in book form.

AVON BOOKS
A division of
The Hearst Corporation
1790 Broadway
New York, New York 10019

Copyright © 1981 by Catherine Edwards Sadler
Text illustrations Copyright © 1981 by Andrew Glass
Cover illustration by Howard Levitt
Book design by Joyce Kubat
Published by arrangement with the author
Library of Congress Catalog Card Number: 81-65084
ISBN: 0-380-78105-0

First Camelot Printing, November, 1981

Sadler, Catherine Edwards.
  Sir Arthur Conan Doyle's The Adventures of Sherlock Holmes.
  (An Avon Camelot book)
  Contents: Bk. 1. A study in scarlet. The red-headed league. The man
with the twisted lip — Bk. 2. The sign of the four. The adventure of the
blue carbuncle. The adventure of the speckled band — Bk. 3. The
adventure of the engineer's thumb. The adventure of the beryl
coronet. The adventure of silver blaze. The adventure of the Musgrave
ritual — [etc.]
  1. Detective and mystery stories, American.
2. Children's stories, American. [1. Mystery and detective stories.
2. Short stories] I. Glass, Andrew, ill.

II. Doyle, Arthur Conan, Sir, 1859-1930. Adventures of Sherlock
Holmes. III. Title. IV. Title: Adventures of Sherlock Holmes.
PZ7.S1238Si   [Fic]   81-65084
                          AACR2

Table of Contents

Introduction

Sir Arthur Conan Doyle was born in Edinburgh, Scotland, on May 22, 1859. In 1876 he entered the Edinburgh Medical College as a student of medicine. There he met a certain professor named Joseph Bell. Bell enjoyed amusing his students in a most unusual way. He would tell them a patient's medical and personal history before the patient had uttered a single word! He would observe the exact appearance of the patient and note the smallest detail about him: marks on his hands, stains on his clothing, the jewelry he wore. He would observe a tattoo, a new gold chain, a worn hat with unusual stains upon it. From these *observations* he would then make *deductions*. In other words, he would come to conclusions by reasoning in a logical manner. For example, a tattoo and the way a man walked could lead to the deduction that the man had been to sea; a new gold chain could lead to the deduction that he had come into recent wealth. Time and time again Professor Bell's deductions proved correct!

Conan Doyle was intrigued by Professor Bell's skills of observation and deduction. Since his early youth he had been fascinated by the mysterious. He loved mysteries and detective stories. He himself had already tried his hand at writing. Now a new sort of hero began to take shape in Conan Doyle's mind. His hero would be a detective—not just an ordinary detective, though. No, he would be extraordinary . . . a man like Bell who observed the smallest detail. He would take his skills of observation and work them out to an exact science—the science of deduction. "It is all very well to say that a man is clever," Conan Doyle wrote, "but the reader wants to see examples of it—such examples as Bell gave us every day. . . ." So Conan Doyle created just such a clever man, a man who had perfected the skill of observation, turned it into an exact science, and then used it as the basis of his career. His cleverness would be revealed in the extraordinary methods he used to solve his cases and capture his criminals.

Little by little the personality and world of his new character took shape. At last he became the sharp-featured fellow we all know as Mr. Sherlock Holmes. Next Conan Doyle turned his imagination to Holmes' surroundings—those "comfortable rooms in Baker Street"—where the fire was always blazing and where footsteps were always heard on the stair. And then there was Watson, dear old Watson! He was much like Conan Doyle himself, easygoing, typically British, a doctor and a writer. Watson would be Holmes' sidekick, his friend and his chronicler. He would be humble and admiring, always asking Holmes to explain his theories, always ready to go out into the foggy, gaslit streets of London on some mysterious mission. All that remained to create were the adventures themselves.

Taking up his pen in 1886, Conan Doyle set to work on a short novel, or novella as it is sometimes called. He finished *A Study in Scarlet* in just two months. It was the first of sixty Sherlock Holmes stories to come and it began a career for Dr. Arthur Conan Doyle that would eventually win him a knighthood.

Today Holmes is considered one of—if not *the*—most popular fictional heroes of all time. More has been written about this character than any other. Sherlock Holmes societies have been created, plays and movies based on the detective have been made, a castle in Switzerland houses a Sherlock Holmes collection, a tavern in London bears his name and features a reconstruction of his rooms in Baker Street. He has even been poked fun at and been called everything from Picklock Holes to Hemlock Jones!

Why such a fuss over a character who appeared in a series of stories close to a century ago? Elementary, dear reader! He is loved. He is loved for his genius, his coolness, his individuality, and for the safety he represents. For as long as Sherlock Holmes is alive the world is somehow safe. The villains will be outsmarted and good and justice will win out. And so he has been kept alive these hundred years by readers around the globe. And since today we are still in need of just such a clever hero it seems a safe deduction that Mr. Sherlock Holmes—and his dear old Watson—will go on living in these pages for a good many more years to come.

The Adventure of the Engineer's Thumb

The Adventure of the Engineer's Thumb is one of the more gruesome adventures of Sherlock Holmes.

The engineer of the title is a hydraulic engineer, which means he specializes in machinery that runs by liquid (usually water) which is under tremendous pressure. It is a field which we tend to think of as being modern and yet here we find a fellow in the 1880's with just such a speciality. A hydraulic press is commonly used to compress objects. Its force is immense and it is thus most often used to combine and compress metals. It is for this reason that the engineer of the story is wary of its use as a machine to compress soft "fuller's earth."

The Adventure of
the Engineer's Thumb

"The Adventure of the Engineer's Thumb" was one of the few mysteries which I brought to Sherlock Holmes' attention. It occurred in the summer of 1889, not long after my marriage. I had returned to medical practice and no longer lived with Holmes on Baker Street. My practice was located near the train station and I often treated railway officials. One man in particular was very grateful to me for curing him from a painful disease. He was a railway guard and was always sending me new patients.

One morning I was awakened by the maid tapping at the door. She announced that there were two men waiting for me in my office. I dressed quickly and rushed downstairs. As I came down the stairs the guard was just leaving the office.

"I've got him in there," he whispered. "He's all right."

"What is it then?" I asked. The way he spoke I thought he had caged some strange creature in my room.

"It's a new patient," he whispered. "I thought I'd bring him to you myself. I didn't want him to slip away. There he is, all safe and sound. I must go now, Doctor, I have my duties, same as you." And off he went.

I entered my office. I found a gentleman seated by the table. He was quietly dressed in a tweed suit. He had laid his soft cloth cap upon the table. A handkerchief was wrapped around one of his hands. It was stained all over with blood. He was young—no more than twenty-five. He had a strong, masculine face. He was terribly pale and looked extraordinarily upset.

"I am sorry to disturb you so early in the morning, Doctor," said he. "But I have had a very serious accident during the night. I came in by train this morning. At the station I inquired as to where I might find a doctor. The guard very kindly brought me to you. I gave the maid my business card, but I see that she has left it upon the table."

I picked it up and glanced at it: MR. VICTOR HATHERLEY, HYDRAULIC ENGINEER, 16A VICTORIA STREET (3rd FLOOR). "I regret that I kept you waiting," I said and sat down in my chair. "You are fresh from a night journey. That is usually both dull and tiring."

"Oh, my night could not be called dull!" he said. He began to laugh. His voice became shrill and his sides shook terribly.

"Stop it!" I cried. "Pull yourself together, man!" I poured him a glass of water, but he seemed out of control. It was quite some time before he calmed himself down.

"I have been making a fool of myself," he gasped.

"Not at all. Drink this!" I dashed some brandy into the water. As he drank, the color began to come back to his bloodless cheeks.

"That's better!" the engineer said. "And now, Doctor, perhaps you would look at my thumb or rather the place where my thumb used to be."

He unwound his handkerchief and held out his hand. I shuddered to look at it. There were four normal fingers and a horrid red spongy area where the thumb should have been. It had been hacked or torn right out from its roots!

"Good heavens," I cried. "This is a terrible injury. It must have bled a great deal."

"Yes, it did. I fainted when it was done. I must have been senseless for some time. When I came to, I found that it was still bleeding. So I tied one end of my handkerchief very tightly around my wrist and braced it with a twig."

"Excellent!" I said. I examined the wound more closely. "This has been done by a very heavy and sharp instrument," I commented.

"A thing like a cleaver," he said.

"An accident, I presume?"

"By no means," he replied.

"What! A murderous attack?!" I exclaimed.

"Very murderous indeed."

"You horrify me."

I sponged the wound, cleaned it, and bandaged it. He lay back without wincing, though he bit his lip from time to time.

"How is that?" I asked when I had finished.

"Fine! Between your brandy and your bandages I feel like a new man. I was very weak, but I have gone through a great deal."

"Perhaps you had better not speak of the matter," I said. "It is obviously very upsetting to you."

"Oh no, not now. I shall have to tell my tale to the police. Between ourselves, they would probably not believe my story were it not for this wound. It is really quite extraordinary and I have little proof to back me up. Even if they do believe me, the chances that justice will be done are slim. I have only vague clues to give them."

"Ha!" cried I. "If it is a problem which needs solving

then I recommend you see my friend Mr. Sherlock Holmes."

"Oh, I have heard of the fellow," answered my visitor. "I should be very glad to consult him ... although I shall have to go to the police as well. Would you write me a reference?"

"I'll do better. I'll take you around to him myself."

"I should be immensely obliged to you," the engineer said.

"We'll call a cab and go together. We shall just be in time to have a little breakfast with him. Do you feel up to it?"

"Yes, I shall not feel easy until I have told my story."

"Then my servant will call a cab and I shall be with you in an instant." I rushed upstairs, explained the matter to my wife, and in five minutes we were in a hansom cab driving to Baker Street.

As I expected, Sherlock Holmes was up. He was in his dressing gown and was smoking his before-breakfast pipe. He seemed pleased to see us, ordered fresh rashers of bacon and eggs, and joined us in a hearty meal. When we were through we settled the engineer upon the sofa. We placed a pillow behind his head and laid a glass of brandy and water within his reach.

"It is clear that you have had an extraordinary experience," Holmes said. "Please lie down there and make yourself at home. Tell us what you can but stop when you are tired. Keep up your strength with the brandy and water."

"Thank you," said my patient. "But I have felt another man since the doctor bandaged me. I think your breakfast has completed the cure. I shall take up as little of your valuable time as possible, so I shall start my peculiar story at once."

Holmes sat in his big armchair while I sat opposite him, as we listened in silence to the strange story of the engineer.

"You must know," he started, "that I am an orphan and a bachelor. I live alone here in London. By profession I am an engineer. I have had considerable experience at my work during the seven years I worked for a well-known firm in Greenwich. Two years ago I came into some money after my poor father's death. I decided to go into business for myself and rented an office in Victoria Street.

"I suppose the start of any business is difficult. I have had few jobs these past two years. I have earned little. Every day from nine in the morning until four in the afternoon I wait in my office for customers. I was beginning to think that my venture had failed.

"Then yesterday my clerk entered to say that a gentleman wished to see me on business. He brought up a business card with the name 'Colonel Lysander Stark' engraved upon it. Close at his heels came Colonel Stark. He was a tall man but terribly thin. I do not think that I have ever seen such a thin man. He was plainly but neatly dressed and his age seemed to be nearer forty than thirty.

" 'Mr. Hatherley?' said he, with something of a German accent. 'You have been recommended to me, Mr. Hatherley. I have been told that you are both good at your profession and able to keep a secret.'

"I bowed, feeling quite flattered. 'May I ask who gave you such a good reference?' I asked.

" 'Well, perhaps it is better if I not tell you just yet. The same source told me that you are both an orphan and a bachelor, and live alone in London.'

" 'That is quite correct,' I answered, 'although I do not see what that has to do with my work. It *is* about work that you have come?'

" 'Yes, indeed. But you will soon see that everything I say is to the point. I have a job for you of absolute secrecy and of course you can expect that more from a single man than one who lives with a large family.'

" 'If I promise to keep a secret, I shall keep it,' I said.

" 'You do promise then?' he asked.

" 'Yes, I promise.'

" 'You will keep absolute and complete silence, before, during, and after? You will not say or write a word about this matter?'

" 'I have already given you my word.'

" 'Very good.' He suddenly sprang up and rushed over to the door. He opened it quickly. The corridor was empty.

" 'That's all right,' he said, coming back. 'I know how clerks are sometimes curious about their boss's affairs.' He pulled up his chair very close to mine and stared at me in a questioning way.

"I was beginning to feel repulsed by the man. Something about his manner made me afraid.

" 'I beg that you state your business, sir.' I said. 'My time is of value.'

" 'How would fifty guineas for a night's work suit you?' he asked.

" 'Most admirably,' I said. That was ten times my usual fee.

" 'I say a night's work, but it's more like an hour. I

simply want your opinion about a hydraulic machine that has got out of gear. If you show us what is wrong we shall soon set it right ourselves. What do you think of such a job?'

" 'The work appears light, and the pay generous.'

" 'Precisely so. We shall want you to come tonight by the last train.'

" 'Where to?' I asked.

" 'To Eyford, in Berkshire. There is a train which arrives at Eyford at eleven-fifteen.'

" 'Very good,' I said.

" 'I shall come down in a carriage to meet you.'

" 'There is a drive then?'

" 'Yes, our little place is out in the country. It is a good seven miles from Eyford Station.'

" 'Then we can hardly get there before midnight. I suppose there will be no chance of a train back that night. I should have to stay over.'

" 'Yes, we could easily put you up,' the Colonel said.

" 'That is very awkward. Could I not come at a more convenient hour?'

" 'We think it best for you to come late. That is why we are paying you such a high salary. There is still time for you to back out.'

"I thought of the fifty guineas and of how useful the money would be. 'Not at all,' said I. 'I shall be very happy to do as you wish. I should like to understand better what you wish me to do.'

" 'Quite so,' he responded. 'It is natural that you should be curious about such a secret matter. You should know everything before you take on the job. Are we absolutely safe from eavesdroppers?'

" 'Entirely,' I answered.

" 'You have probably heard about fuller's earth. It is a claylike substance that is used in many ways—most importantly to purify and refine oils. It is a very valuable product and is only found in one or two places in England.'

" 'Yes, I have heard this.'

" 'Some time ago I bought a small place in the country. I discovered there was a deposit of this fuller's earth in one of my fields. I soon found that my deposit was really very small—however, it was linked to two larger deposits on either side. Both were located on my neighbors' land. My neighbors had no idea their land contained something so valuable. Naturally, it was in my interest to buy their land before they discovered its true value. Unfortunately, I had no money. I took a few friends into my secret. They suggested that we quietly and secretly work our own little deposit. Soon we would earn enough money to buy the neighboring land. We have been working our deposit for some time now. To help us in our work we bought a hydraulic press—a machine to compact the earth. It has gone out of order and that is why I have come to you. We guard our secret jealously. Someone might suspect if they knew an engineer was coming to our house. That is why you must come late at night. I hope it is clear to you!'

" 'Yes, I understand,' I said. 'The only point I'm not clear on is what use you have with a hydraulic press. It is my understanding that fuller's earth is dug out of the ground like gravel from a pit.'

" 'Ah!' said he, carelessly, 'we have our own process. We compress the earth into bricks. This way we can remove them without revealing what they are. But that is mere detail. I have now taken you fully into my confidence, Mr.

Hatherley!' He rose as he spoke. 'I shall expect you at Eyford at 11:15.'

" 'I shall certainly be there,' said I.

" 'And not a word to a soul.' He shook my hand and hurried from the room.

"Well, I was quite astonished at this new turn of events. On the one hand, I was glad because fifty guineas was ten times my usual pay. On the other hand, there was something unpleasant about the man. His explanation of the fuller's earth and the reason for going so late did not sit right with me. Still, I had given my word. I ate a hearty supper, drove to the station, and boarded the train for Eyford.

"I arrived in Eyford a little after eleven o'clock. I was the only passenger who got out. There was only a sleepy porter on the platform. As I passed the gate, I spotted Colonel Stark. He was waiting in the shadows. He grasped my arm and pulled me into the carriage. He closed the windows and told the driver to go."

"One horse?" interrupted Holmes.

"Yes, only one."

"Did you observe the color?" Holmes asked.

"Yes, it was chestnut," the engineer answered.

"Tired-looking or fresh?"

"Oh, fresh and glossy."

"Thank you," said Holmes. "I am sorry to have interrupted you. Please continue your most interesting statement."

"Away we went then and drove at least an hour. Colonel Lysander Stark said that it was seven miles. But from the time it took, I'd say it was closer to twelve. The Colonel sat next to me and did not speak. I tried to look out the window, but it was frosted and I could not see through it. The road was bumpy although we did not go up any hills. We lurched and jolted terribly. At last the bumping stopped and the ride became smooth. We were driving over a gravel driveway. Then the carriage came to a standstill. We stepped out of the carriage and right onto a porch. I was unable to see the front of the house. The door was slammed immediately shut behind us. I heard the rattle of the carriage wheels as it drove away.

"It was pitch dark inside the house. The Colonel fumbled with his matches. Suddenly a door opened at the other end of the passage. A long golden bar of light shot out in our direction. A woman appeared with a lamp in her hand. I could see that she was pretty and her dress was of some rich material. She spoke a few words in a foreign language. The Colonel answered her gruffly. She gave such a start at his reply that the lamp nearly fell out of her hand. Colonel Stark took the lamp from her, whispered something in her ear, and pushed her back into the room from whence she came.

" 'If you will please wait in this room,' Stark said, opening another door. It was a quiet little room with a round table in its center. Several books were scattered on it. Colonel Stark laid the lamp down on the table. 'I shall return in an instant,' he said and vanished in the darkness.

"I glanced at the books. Although I do not speak the language, I could tell that they were in German. I walked across to the window, hoping to catch a glimpse of the countryside. But the window was covered by a barred oak shutter. An old clock ticked loudly in the passage, but otherwise the house was deadly still. A feeling of uneasiness crept over me. Who were these German people?

What were they doing in this strange, out-of-the-way place? And where was this place? All I knew was that I was ten miles or so from Eyford. But in which direction: north, east, south, west? I had no idea.

"Suddenly the door of my room swung open. There stood the woman. She seemed sick with fear. She held up a shaking finger to warn me to be silent. Then she spoke a few words in broken English. As she spoke she kept glancing into the gloom behind her.

" 'I would go,' said she. 'I should not stay here. There is no good for you here!'

" 'But, madam,' I said, 'I have not yet done my work. I cannot leave until I have seen the machine.'

" 'It is not worth your while to wait,' she went on. 'You can pass through the door. No one will stop you.' I smiled and shook my head 'no.' She stepped forward and clasped her hands together. 'For the love of heaven!' she whispered. 'Get away before it is too late!'

"But I have a stubborn nature. I thought of my high fee, and the long ride to Eyford. Was it all for nothing? Why should I flee without having done my job or gotten paid? For all I knew this woman could be crazy. She was about to plead with me some more, when she heard steps on the stair. She vanished as quickly as she had appeared.

"The newcomers were Colonel Stark and a short, fat man with a heavy beard. He was introduced to me as Mr. Ferguson.

" 'This is my secretary and manager,' said the Colonel. 'Funny, I thought I left this door shut just now. I hope you haven't felt a draught.'

" 'On the contrary,' I said, 'I opened the door myself as I was feeling a bit warm.'

"He looked at me suspiciously. 'Perhaps we had better proceed to business,' he said. 'Mr. Ferguson and I will take you up to see the machine.'

" 'I had better put on my hat then,' I said.

" 'That won't be necessary. The machine is here,' the Colonel said.

" 'What? You dig fuller's earth right in the house?'

" 'No, no. This is only where we compress it,' he answered. 'But never mind that! All we wish you to do is examine the machine and tell what is wrong with it.'

"We went upstairs together. The Colonel went first with the lamp, then the fat manager, and I behind him. We walked through corridors, passages, winding staircases. There were no carpets, and no signs of any furniture above the first floor. The plaster was peeling off the walls, and the damp was breaking through in green, unhealthy blotches. I did not forget the lady's warning and watched my two companions closely.

"At last Colonel Lysander Stark stopped at a very low door. He unlocked it. Within was a small, square room. It was so small that the three of us could not fit inside. Ferguson remained outside, while the Colonel ushered me in.

" 'We are now,' he said, 'actually inside the press. It would be very unpleasant for us if someone were to turn it on. The ceiling of this small room is the bottom of the press. It comes down with many tons of force upon this metal floor. The machine still works, but there is some stiffness in it. Perhaps you could look it over and show us how to set it right.'

"I took the lamp from him and examined the machine thoroughly. It was a gigantic one and capable of exerting enormous pressure. I went outside and examined the levers which controlled it. I saw at once what was wrong. One of the india rubber bands around the head of a driving rod had shrunk. This was causing a loss of power. I pointed this out to the two men. They listened carefully to me and asked me several practical questions. After I made it clear to them, I returned to the chamber. I wanted to satisfy my curiosity. I knew that the story of the fuller's earth was a lie . . . it was absurd to think that so powerful a machine could be used for stamping earth. The walls were wood but the floor was iron. When I examined the floor, I found that there was a metallic crust all over it. I stooped down and scraped at it. There could be no doubt they were compressing metal. Suddenly I heard the German exclaim.

" 'What are you doing there?' he asked.

"I felt angry at having been tricked by his story. 'I was admiring your fuller's earth,' said I. 'I think I could advise you better, if I knew the real work you are doing with this machine.'

"The instant I said these words, I regretted them. Stark's face turned hard and his eyes turned mean.

" 'Very well,' said he. 'You shall know all about this machine.' He took a step backward, slammed the little door, and turned the key. I rushed toward it and pulled the handle. It would not move. I kicked it and shoved it, but it was no use. I was locked in. 'Hullo!' I yelled. 'Let me out!'

"And then suddenly a loud noise pierced the silence. He had turned on the machine. The lamp still stood on the floor. By its light I saw the black ceiling begin to move. It was slowly, jerkily coming down on me. In a minute it would grind me to a shapeless pulp! I threw myself against the door and screamed. I dragged my nails across the lock.

I begged the Colonel to let me out. The ceiling kept coming down, lower and lower. I raised my hand and could feel its rough surface moving closer. Then I realized that the pain of my death would depend on my position. If I lay on my face the weight would come on my spine. I shuddered to think of that dreadful snap. It would be easier to let it strike my head. But did I have the courage to look at it as it came down upon me? I scanned the room for some last ray of hope. Miraculously, I found it!

"I saw a thin line of yellow light coming from between two wall boards. It broadened and broadened as someone pushed the panel back. For an instant I could hardly believe my eyes. Here was an opening to safety! The next moment I had thrown myself through the opening and lay half-fainting on the other side. The panel was closed behind me. I could hear the crash of the lamp and the clang of the ceiling and floor meeting. I knew then how close my escape had been.

"I found myself lying upon a stone floor in a narrow corridor. The beautiful woman was bending over me. She tugged at me with her left hand. Her right held up a candle.

" 'Come! come!' she cried. 'They will be here in a moment. They will see that you are not there. Oh, do not waste the precious time. Come!'

"This time I listened to her advice. I staggered to my feet and we ran together along the corridor and down a winding stair. This led to a broad passage. Just as we reached it we heard the sound of running feet. The two men were close on our heels. My guide looked about her frantically. Then she threw open a door. It led into a bedroom. Through its window I could see the full moon.

" 'It's your only chance,' she said, pointing to the window. 'It is high, but maybe you can jump it.'

"As she spoke a light came into view at the other end of the passage. I suddenly saw the lean figure of Colonel Lysander Stark. He was rushing toward us with a lantern in one hand and a weapon like a butcher's cleaver in the other. I ran across the bedroom, flung open the window, and looked out. The garden below was no more than thirty feet down. I climbed out onto the sill, but I hesitated to jump. I wanted to hear what would pass between my savior and the Colonel. If he hurt her, I would go back to assist her at any risk to me. I had just thought this when he was at the door, pushing his way past her. She threw her arms around him and tried to hold him back.

" 'Fritz! Fritz!' she cried in English. 'Remember your promise last time. You said it should not be again. He will be silent! Oh, he will be silent!'

" 'You are mad, Elise!' he shouted and tried to break away from her. 'You will be the ruin of us. He has seen too much. Let me pass, I say.' He shoved her to one side and rushed to the window. He cut at me with his heavy weapon. I had let myself go and was hanging by my hands when his blow fell. I could feel a dull pain. My grip loosened and I fell into the garden below

"I was shaken, but I was not hurt by the fall. So I picked myself up and rushed toward some rose bushes for shelter. Suddenly I became dizzy and sick. My hand was throbbing painfully. I glanced down at it. My thumb had been cut off! Blood was pouring from the wound. I tried to tie my handkerchief around it, but suddenly there was a buzzing in my ears. I fainted among the rose bushes.

"I do not know how long I remained there. It must have been a long time because the moon was gone and a bright morning was breaking when I came to. My clothes were wet from dew and my coat sleeve was drenched with blood from my wounded thumb. The pain of it reminded me of last night's adventure. I sprang to my feet, sure that I was still not safe. To my astonishment, I was no longer in the garden. I had been lying near a hedge by the high road. A low building was close by. I walked over to it. It was Eyford Station.

"Half dazed, I went into the station and asked about the morning train. I had less than an hour to wait. The same porter from the night before was on duty. I asked him whether he had ever heard of Colonel Lysander Stark. He had not. Had he noticed a carriage waiting for me last night? No, he had not. Was there a police station near? There was one three miles off.

"I was too weak and ill to go that far. I decided to wait until I got back to town before telling my story to the police. It was a little past six when I arrived here. So I went straight to have my wound looked at, and the doctor kindly brought me to you. I now put the case in your hands. I shall do exactly what you advise."

For a moment both of us were silent. Then Sherlock Holmes pulled a huge scrapbook down from his shelf.

"Here is an advertisement that will interest you," he said to the engineer. "It appeared in all the papers about a year ago. Listen to this:

LOST ON THE 9TH OF THIS MONTH, MR. JEREMIAH HAYLING, AGED 26, AN ENGINEER. LEFT HIS LODGINGS AT TEN O'CLOCK AT

NIGHT AND HAS NOT BEEN HEARD OF
SINCE. WAS DRESSED IN . . .

etc., etc. Ha! This was the last time the Colonel needed his
machine fixed, I fancy."

"Good heavens!" cried my patient. "Then that explains
what the girl said about Stark's promise."

"Yes. It is quite clear that the Colonel was a cool and
desperate man. It seems nothing could stand in the way of
his little game. Well, every moment now is precious. If you
are well enough, let us go to Scotland Yard. From there we
will return to Eyford."

Some three hours or so later we were all in the train
together. There were Sherlock Holmes, the engineer,
Inspector Bradstreet of Scotland Yard, a plain-clothes man,
and myself. Bradstreet had spread a map of the area out on
the seat. He was now busy drawing a circle around Eyford.

"There you are," he said. "That circle is drawn at a ten
mile radius around the village. The place we are looking
for must be within that circle. You said ten miles, I think,
sir?"

"It was a good hour's drive," answered the engineer.

"And you think they brought you back all that way
when you were unconscious?" the Inspector asked.

"They must have done. I have a confused memory of
being lifted and moved."

"What I cannot understand," I said, "is why they
spared your life when they found you lying in the garden.
Perhaps the woman's pleas had softened the villain's
heart."

"I hardly think that likely. I never saw such a strong-
willed face in all my life," my patient responded.

"Oh, we shall soon clear it all up," said Bradstreet. "Well, I have drawn the circle. I only wish I knew at what point in it we can find these people."

"I think I could lay my finger on it," said Holmes quietly.

"Really now!" cried the Inspector. "You have formed an opinion! Come now, we shall see who agrees with you. I say it is south, for the country is more deserted there."

"And I say east," said my patient.

"I am for west," remarked the plain-clothes man. "There are several quiet villages up there."

"And I am for the north," said I. "Because there are no hills there and our friend said he didn't notice the carriage go up any."

"Come," cried the Inspector, laughing. "Who do you vote for?"

"You are all wrong," said Holmes.

"But we can't *all* be wrong."

"Oh yes, you can." Holmes placed his finger at the center of the circle. "This is where we shall find them."

"But the twelve mile drive?" gasped Hatherley.

"Six out and six back. Nothing simpler. You say your horse was fresh and glossy when you got in. How could it be if it had gone twelve miles over heavy roads?"

"Indeed, it seems a likely trick," observed Bradstreet thoughtfully. "Of course, there can be no doubt as to the nature of this gang."

"None at all," said Holmes. "They are counterfeiters. They make fake coins on a large scale. They work the machine to combine metals they use instead of silver."

"We have known for a long time that a clever gang of counterfeiters were at work. They are turning out thousands of coins. We even traced them to hereabouts. But they covered their tracks well. Now, thanks to this lucky chance, I think we have finally got them."

But the Inspector was mistaken. These criminals were not destined to fall into the hands of justice. As we rolled into the Eyford Station we saw a gigantic column of smoke. It came from behind a clump of trees nearby.

"A house on fire?" asked Bradstreet, when we were off the train.

"Yes, sir!" said the station master.

"When did it break out?"

"I hear that it was during the night, sir. But it has got worse. The whole place is ablaze."

"Whose house is it?"

"Dr. Becher's," the station master replied.

"Tell me," broke in the engineer, "is Dr. Becher a German and very thin with a long sharp nose?"

The station master laughed heartily. "No sir, Dr. Becher is an Englishman and he's fatter than most! But he has a gentleman staying with him who I understand is a foreigner and he looks like some good local beef would do him no harm."

We thanked the station master and we rushed toward the fire. There was a great white-washed house in front of us. Fire was pouring out from every chink and window. Three fire engines were trying to gain control of it from the garden in front.

"That's it!" cried Hatherley. "There is the gravel drive, and there are the rose bushes where I lay. That second window is the one I jumped from!"

"Well, at least you have had your revenge on them,"

said Holmes. "There can be no question that it was your oil lamp which set the fire. You said that you placed a lantern on the floor of the press when you were examining it. When the ceiling came crashing down on it, it must have set fire to its wooden walls. The villains were too busy chasing you to notice it. Now look for your friends in the crowd, though I fear they are a good hundred miles away by now."

Holmes' fears were correct. From that day to this there has been no word of the beautiful woman, the sinister German, or the fat Englishman. Early that morning someone passed a cart containing several people and some very bulky boxes. They were driving furiously down the road. That was the last anyone saw of them. Even Holmes was unable to discover any clues to their whereabouts.

The firemen were baffled by the strange machine they found within . . . and even more so by the human thumb they found upon the second floor windowsill. Their efforts to squash the fire were of no use, and the house burned to the ground. All that was left were some charred machinery and large masses of tin and nickel. But no coins were found. They were obviously packed away in those bulky boxes.

How the engineer was taken from the garden to the road would have remained a mystery forever. But the soft earth told us the end of the story. He had been carried by two persons, one with remarkably small feet and the other with unusually large ones. The silent Englishman must have been less murderous than the German, and helped the woman drag the engineer out of danger's way.

"Well," said our engineer as we traveled back to

London, "I have lost my thumb, and my fee! What have I gained by this?"

"Experience," said Holmes, laughing. "And your adventure may prove of value to you yet. Put it into words and you have a tale truly worth telling. You may not have profited from it financially, but you will be a most entertaining guest for the rest of your life!"

The
Adventure
of the
Beryl
Coronet

The coronet of the title is not to be confused with a cornet—a musical wind instrument. A coronet is a small crown worn by princes and other high-ranking nobles. A coronation is a ceremony at which just such a crown or coronet is placed upon the head of a king or queen.

This adventure points up Conan Doyle's tendency to be perplexing at times. He clearly states at the beginning of the story that there would be a great public scandal were any harm to come to the coronet. The story revolves around recovering the lost crown. When it is finally recovered it is both twisted and torn. Yet Holder thanks Holmes for preventing a great public scandal! Has Conan Doyle ended the story purposely on this puzzling note or has he simply slipped up? Let the reader be the final judge. *The Adventure of the Beryl Coronet* remains a thoroughly exciting mystery in which Holmes once again shows us how truly clever he is!

The Adventure of the Beryl Coronet

One morning when I was still living on Baker Street, I stood looking out our window. "Holmes," I said, "here comes a madman. It seems rather sad that his relatives allow him to go out alone."

My friend rose lazily from his armchair. He walked over to me and looked out. It was a bright, crisp February morning. The snow from the night before still lay on the ground. The street was empty except for the man I spoke of. He was about fifty years of age, tall and broad. He had a strong face and a commanding figure. He was dressed in a serious but rich style. He wore a black frock coat, a shiny hat, neat brown shoes, and well-cut gray trousers. Yet, this man seemed anything but dignified, for he was running down the street. Every once in a while he would sort of skip, as though his legs weren't used to the running. He jerked his hands up and down and wiggled his head in a most extraordinary way.

"What on earth can be the matter with him?" I asked. "He is looking at the house numbers."

"I believe he is coming here," said Sherlock Holmes, rubbing his hands.

"Here?"

"Yes, I rather think he is coming here to consult me professionally. I think I recognize the symptoms. Ha! Didn't I tell you?"

At that moment the man came puffing and blowing to

our door. He pulled our bell so hard that the clang rang throughout the house.

A few moments later he was standing in our room. There was such a look of grief and despair in his eyes that our smiles were turned instantly to horror and pity. He was so upset that he could not speak. His whole body swayed back and forth and his hands plucked frantically at his hair. Then suddenly he sprang to his feet and beat his head against the wall. We both rushed toward him and pulled him into the center of the room. Holmes pushed him into an easy chair and began to speak with him soothingly.

"You have come to tell me your story, haven't you?" Holmes said. "You are tired from rushing so. Please wait until you have rested, then I shall be most happy to look into any little problem you may have."

The man sat for a minute or more. His chest was heaving and he had to fight back the emotion. Then he wiped his brow with his handkerchief, set his lips tight, and turned to us.

"No doubt you think me mad?" said he.

"I see you have some great trouble," responded Holmes.

"God knows I have! The trouble is enough to drive me mad. I could have faced public disgrace, although I have never done anything to be ashamed of. And every man has some private grief in his life. . . . But to have to suffer public disgrace and private grief at once is too much! And for it to come in so frightful a form! It shakes me to my soul! Besides, I am not the only one who is affected. The noblest in the land will suffer unless there is some way out of this horrible affair!"

"Please take hold of yourself, sir," said Holmes. "Now

let me have a clear account of who you are and what has happened to you."

"My name," answered our visitor, "is probably familiar to your ears. I am Alexander Holder, of the banking firm of Holder & Stevenson, of Threadneedle Street, London."

The name was indeed familiar to us. He was the senior partner in the second largest private banking concern in London. What could have happened to one of our foremost citizens? We waited in curiosity for him to tell his story.

"I feel that time is of value," said he. "I hastened here from the police station. The police inspector suggested I contact you. I took the Underground and from there hurried on by foot. The cabs go so slowly in this snow. That is why I am so out of breath. But I feel better now and will put the facts before you as clearly as I can.

"As you may know, we in the banking business often give out loans. To obtain a loan a person must put up some form of security. In the event that the loan is not paid back, we then have something of value in exchange. Over the past few years we have lent much money in this way. There are many noble families to whom we have loaned large sums of money. They have used their pictures, their libraries, their silver, and so on as security.

"Yesterday morning I was seated at my office at the bank when one of my clerks brought me a business card. I was startled at the name on it. It was none other than—well, perhaps even to you I should only say that his name is known all over the earth. It is one of the highest, noblest, most respected names in England. I was over-whelmed by the honor of his visit. I attempted to say so when he entered, but he plunged right away into business.

" 'Mr. Holder,' he said. 'I have been informed that you loan money.'

" 'Yes, we do, when the security is good,' I answered.

" 'It is absolutely essential,' said he, 'that I have fifty thousand pounds at once. I could of course borrow so small a sum from my friends. But I prefer to make this a matter of business ... and to carry out that business myself. In my position, it is unwise to place myself in other peoples' debt.'

" 'For how long do you want the sum?' I asked.

" 'Next Monday I shall be receiving a large sum of money. I shall then most certainly repay the money you advance—with whatever interest you think is right to charge. But is is very important that the money be loaned to me at once.' He pulled out a square, black leather case. 'You have doubtless heard of the Beryl Coronet?' he said.

" 'One of the most precious crowns in all England,' I answered.

" 'Precisely.' He opened the case. There, embedded in soft, flesh-colored velvet, lay the crown. The green-blue of the shining gems dazzled my eyes. 'There are thirty-nine enormous beryls,' said he. 'We can only guess at the price of the gold casing. The lowest estimate would put it at double the sum I am asking. I am prepared to leave it with you as my security.'

"I took the precious case in my hands and looked nervously from it to my illustrious client.

" 'You doubt its value?' he asked.

" 'Not at all. I only doubt—'

" 'Whether it is proper for me to leave it. You may set your mind at rest about it. I shall reclaim the coronet in four days. Is the security enough?'

" 'Yes,' I answered.

" 'You understand, Mr. Holder, that I am trusting you completely. I rely on you not to speak of this matter to anyone. And to guard this coronet with your life. If any harm were to come to it, there would be a public scandal. The crown has been in my family for generations. But as you know, all such treasures truly belong to the nation. Any injury to it would be almost as serious as its complete loss. There are no beryls in the world to match these. It would be impossible to replace them. I leave it with you. I shall call for it in person on Monday morning.'

"I could see that my client was anxious to leave. I called for my cashier and ordered him to hand over fifty thousand-pound notes. As soon as I was alone, I began to have misgivings about the entire affair. The care of such a national treasure was a great responsibility. However, there was nothing to be done now. So, I locked it up in my private safe and returned to work.

"When evening came, I felt it unsafe to leave such a precious thing in the office. Banker's safes have been broken into before. If mine were broken into I would be in a terrible position. I decided, therefore, that for the next few days I would always keep the case near me. I called a cab and drove out to my house with the case in my pocket. I did not breathe freely until I had taken it upstairs and locked it in the bureau of my dressing room.

"And now I must tell you about my household, Mr. Holmes. I have three maidservants who have been with me a number of years. They are completely trustworthy and above suspicion. I have a fourth maid who has only worked for me a few months. She came with excellent references, however, and I have been pleased with her work. She is a very pretty girl and has attracted many admirers. They sometimes hang about the place. That is her only drawback, but we believe her to be a thoroughly good girl in every way.

"So much for the servants. My family is so small that it won't take long to describe it. I am a widower and have only one son, Arthur. He is a terrible disappointment, Mr. Holmes. No doubt I have no one to blame but myself. People tell me that I spoiled him. Very likely I did. When my dear wife died I felt that he was all I had to love. I could not bear to see the smile fade from his face. I have never refused him anything he wanted. Perhaps, it would have been better for us both, had I been stricter.

"I wanted him to go into my business, but he was not business-minded. He was wild, and to speak the truth, I could not trust him with large sums of money. When he was young he joined a club. Many of the members were aristocrats with much money and expensive habits. He learned how to play cards, and squander money at the races. Again and again he had to come to me to advance him his allowance. He was always having to pay back some debt or other. He tried a number of times to break away from these bad people. But his friend, Sir George Burnwell, kept drawing him back again.

"I can understand how this man could have an influence over my son. He has come to the house many times and his manner is charming. He is older than Arthur and is a true man of the world. He has been everywhere and seen everything. He is a brilliant man and is most handsome. But I do not think he is trustworthy, and neither does my little Mary.

"And now there is only Mary to describe. She is my niece. My brother died five years ago and left her alone in the world. I adopted her. I have looked upon her as my daughter ever since. She is a sunbeam in my house—sweet, loving, beautiful, a wonderful manager and housekeeper. She is tender and quiet and gentle. She is my right hand. I do not know what I would do without her. In only one matter has she ever gone against my wishes. Twice my boy has asked her to marry him. He loves her devotedly. But both times she has refused. I think Mary could have drawn him onto the right path. Their marriage could have changed his whole life ... but now! alas! it is too late—forever too late!

"Now, Mr. Holmes, you know the people who live under my roof. I shall continue with my miserable story.

"Last night we decided to have our coffee in the drawing room. It was then that I told Mary and Arthur about the precious treasure under our roof. Of course I did not tell them the name of my client. Lucy Parr had brought us the coffee. I am sure she had left the room. I cannot swear that the door was closed, however. Mary and Arthur were both very interested and wanted to see the famous coronet. But I did not want to disturb it.

" 'Where have you put it?' asked Arthur.

" 'In my own bureau.'

" 'Well, I hope to goodness the house won't get burgled during the night,' he said.

" 'It is locked up,' I answered.

" 'Oh, any old key will fit that bureau,' said Arthur. 'When I was a youngster I opened it myself with a key from the lumber room cupboard.'

"He often had a wild way of talking, so I thought little of what he said. Later, he followed me to my room.

" 'Look here, dad,' he said with his eyes downcast. 'Can you let me have two hundred pounds?'

" 'No, I cannot!' I answered sharply. 'I have been far too generous with you in money matters.'

" 'You have been very kind,' he said. 'But I must have this money—or else I can never show my face at the club again.'

" 'And a very good thing, too!' I cried.

" 'Yes, but you wouldn't have me leave it a dishonored man,' said he. 'I could not bear the disgrace. I must raise the money in some way. If you will not let me have it, then I must try other means!'

"I was very angry at him. This was the third request for money this month. 'You shall not have a penny from me,' I cried. He bowed and left the room without another word.

"When he was gone I unlocked my bureau. The coronet was still there. I locked it up again. Then I went about the house, making sure all the doors and windows were fastened. This is usually Mary's task, but with such a treasure in the house, I thought it best to check everything myself. As I came down the stairs I saw Mary herself at the hall window. She closed and locked it as I approached.

"She looked a bit disturbed. 'Tell me, dad,' said she. 'Did you give Lucy permission to go out tonight?'

" 'Certainly not,' I answered.

" 'She just came in by the kitchen door. She was talking with one of her sweethearts again. This really must be stopped!'

" 'You must speak to her in the morning—or I will—if you prefer. Are you sure everything is locked up?' I asked.

" 'Quite sure, dad.'

" 'Then, goodnight.' I kissed her and went up to my bedroom and was soon asleep.

"I am trying to tell you everything, Mr. Holmes. Please question me on any point that is not clear."

"On the contrary, your statement is most clear," said Holmes.

"I come to a part of the story where it is most important to be so. I am not a very heavy sleeper. About two in the morning I was awakened by some sound in the house. It sounded like a window had been gently closed somewhere. I lay in bed listening. Suddenly, to my horror, there was a distinct sound of footsteps moving softly in the next room. I slipped out of bed and peeped around the corner of my dressing room.

" 'Arthur!' I screamed, 'you villain! you thief! How dare you touch the coronet?'

"My boy was dressed only in his shirt and trousers. He was standing beside the light, holding the coronet in his hands. He appeared to be wrenching at it, or bending it, with all his strength. At my cry he dropped it. He turned pale as death. I snatched the crown up and examined it. One of the golden corners with three beryls in it was missing.

" 'You have destroyed it!' I shouted in rage. 'You have dishonored me forever! Where are the jewels which you have stolen?'

" 'Stolen!' he cried.

" 'Yes, you thief!' I roared and shook him by the shoulder.

" 'There are none missing. There cannot be any missing,' said he.

" 'There are three missing. And you know where they are. Must I call you a liar as well as a thief? Didn't I see you trying to tear off another piece?'

" 'You have called me enough names,' said Arthur. 'I will not stand it any longer. Since you have decided to insult me, I shall not say another word about this business. I will leave your house in the morning and will make my own way in the world.'

" 'You shall leave it in the hands of the police!' I cried. I was half mad with rage and grief. 'I shall have this matter investigated!'

" 'You shall learn nothing from me,' he said passionately. 'If you choose to call the police, then let the police find out what they can.'

"By this time the whole house was astir. Mary was the first to rush into the room. At the sight of the coronet she knew immediately what had happened. With a scream she fell to the ground. I sent the housemaid for the police. I put the investigation into their hands at once. Arthur then asked me whether I was going to charge him with theft. I answered that it was no longer a private matter. The ruined coronet was national property. It was now up to the law.

" 'At least,' said he, 'do not have me arrested at once. Let me leave the house for five minutes.'

" 'So that you may get away? Or perhaps so that you can hide what you've stolen?' cried I. Suddenly I realized what a dreadful position I was in now. I begged him to remember that my honor and the honor of someone far greater was at stake. This theft threatened to cause a national scandal. He could stop it all by telling me what he had done with the three missing stones.

" 'You may as well face it,' I said. 'You have been caught in the act. If you tell us where the beryls are, all will be forgiven and forgotten.'

" 'Keep your forgiveness for those who ask for it,' he

answered. He turned away from me with a sneer. I knew that nothing I could say would sway him. So I called in the Inspector. A search was made of his person, his room and every portion of the house. But the gems were not found. And Arthur would not say another word on the subject. This morning he was taken to a prison cell. I filled out all the necessary forms at the station and then hurried to you. I beg you to use your skill to unravel this matter. The police have openly admitted they can make nothing of it. You may go to any expense which you think necessary. I have already offered a reward of a thousand pounds. My God! What shall I do! I have lost my honor, my gems, and my son in one night. Oh, what shall I do!"

He put his hand on either side of his head and rocked it to and fro.

Sherlock Holmes sat silent for some minutes. His brows were knitted and his eyes were fixed on the fire.

"Do you receive company much?" Holmes asked.

"None, except my partner with his family and once in a while a friend of Arthur's. Sir George Burnwell has visited several times lately. No one else, I think."

"Do you go out much?"

"Arthur does. Mary and I stay home. Neither of us care to go out."

"That is unusual for a young girl," commented Sherlock.

"She has a quiet nature. Besides, she is not so very young. She is four and twenty."

"From what you say, this matter seems to have been a shock to her also," Holmes said.

"Terrible! She is even more upset than I," replied the banker.

"Do either of you have any doubts as to Arthur's guilt?"

"How can we have? I saw him with my own eyes. He had the coronet in his hands!"

"I hardly consider that definite proof. Was the rest of the coronet injured?"

"It was twisted."

"Do you think he might have been trying to straighten it out?"

"God bless you! You are doing what you can for him and for me. But what was he doing there at all? If he was innocent, why didn't he say so?"

"Precisely. And if he were guilty, why didn't he invent a lie? His silence can be taken both ways. What did the police think about the noise which awoke you?" Sherlock Holmes asked.

"They thought it might have been caused by Arthur closing his bedroom door."

"A likely story," said Holmes. "As though a man who is going to perform a robbery would really slam his door! And what did they say about the disappearance of the gems?"

"They are still looking beneath the floor and in the furniture in the hope of finding them."

"Have they thought of looking outside the house?" asked Holmes.

"Yes, they have shown extraordinary energy. The whole garden has been minutely examined."

"My dear sir," said Holmes, "to you, the case appears simple, but to me it seems complex. Consider what is involved by your theory. You suppose that your son came down from his bed. He went—at great risk—into your dressing room, opened your bureau, and took out your coronet. He broke off by sheer force a small portion of it. He then went somewhere else and hid the three gems where no one could find them. After all that he returned with the other thirty-six to a room where he could easily be discovered. Does such a theory seem possible to you?"

"But what other is there?" cried the banker in despair. "If his motives were innocent, why doesn't he explain them?"

"It is our task to find that out," replied Holmes. "Let us go to your house and spend an hour or so looking a bit more closely into the details."

My friend insisted on me coming along, which I did gladly. I was very much interested in the case and deeply stirred by the banker's tale. I confess I was as sure of the banker's son's guilt, as was he. But Holmes' reasoning in such matters was remarkable. If he felt the boy was innocent, I felt sure it must be so. Holmes hardly said a word on the way to the banker's house. He sat with his chin on his breast and his hat drawn over his eyes, sunk in the deepest thought. A short railway journey and a shorter walk brought us to Fairbank, the residence of Mr. Holder.

Fairbank was a good-sized square house of white stone. It stood a little back from the road. A drive and snow-covered lawn stretched in front of the house. On the right side of the house was first a garden and then a narrow path. This path linked the kitchen door to the road and was the tradesmen's entrance. On the left side of the house was a lane which led to the stables. Holmes left us standing at the door and walked slowly around the house. He crossed the front lawn, went down the tradesmen's path, over to the garden, and then into the stable lane. He was gone so long that Mr. Holder and I went into the dining room and waited by a fire. We were sitting there in silence when the door opened. A young lady came in. She had dark hair and eyes and her skin was white. I do not think I have ever seen such deadly paleness in a woman's face. Her lips too were bloodless, but her eyes were flushed from crying. She went straight to her uncle and passed her hand over his head with a sweet womanly caress.

"You have given orders for Arthur to be freed, haven't you, dad?" she asked.

"No, no, my girl. The matter must be totally looked into."

"But I am sure that he is innocent. You know of womanly intuition. I know he has done no harm and that you will be sorry for having acted so harshly."

"Why is he silent then, if he is innocent?" Holder asked.

"Who knows? Perhaps he was so angry that you should suspect him."

"How could I help suspecting him? I actually saw him with the coronet in his hand."

"But he had only picked it up to look at it," she said. "Oh, do take my word for it. He is innocent! Let the matter drop, and say no more. It is so dreadful to think of our poor Arthur in prison."

"I shall never let it drop til the gems are found—never, Mary! I have brought a gentleman down from London to inquire into the whole affair."

"This gentleman?" she asked, facing around to me.

"No, his friend. He wished us to leave him alone. He is around in the stable lane now," said the banker.

"The stable lane?" She raised her dark eyebrows.

"What can he hope to find there? Ah! This, I suppose, is he. I trust, sir, that you will prove my cousin Arthur's innocence."

"I fully share your opinion, and hope we may prove it," replied Holmes. "I believe I have the honor of addressing Miss Mary Holder. Might I ask you a question or two?"

"Please do, sir, if it will help to clear up this horrible affair."

"You heard nothing yourself last night?" asked Sherlock Holmes.

"Nothing, until my uncle began to speak loudly. I heard that, and I came downstairs."

"You shut up the windows and doors the night before. Did you lock all the windows?" Holmes asked.

"Yes."

"Were they all locked this morning?"

"Yes."

"Is it true your maid went out to see her sweetheart last night?"

"Yes, and she brought us our coffee in the drawing room. She may have heard Uncle's remarks about the coronet."

"I see. You think she may have gone out to tell her sweetheart about the coronet and they then planned the robbery."

"But what is the good of all these vague theories," cried the banker. "I told you that I saw Arthur with the coronet in his hand."

"Wait a moment, Mr. Holder. We must come back to that. About this girl, Miss Holder. You saw her return by the kitchen door, I presume?"

"Yes—I went to see if the door was locked for the night. I saw her slipping in. I saw the man too. He was standing in the darkness."

"Do you know him?" Holmes asked.

"Oh, yes. He is the greengrocer who brings our vegetables around. His name is Francis Prosper."

"Did he stand to the left of the door, further up the path?" asked Holmes.

"Yes, he did," she answered.

"And is he a man with a wooden leg?"

Something like fear sprang up in the young lady's eyes. "Why, you are a magician," said she. "How do you know that?" She smiled, but Holmes did not smile back.

"I should like to go upstairs now," he said. "I shall probably wish to go over the outside of the house again. Perhaps I had better take a look at the first floor windows before I go up."

He walked from one window to another. He only paused at the hall window which overlooked the stable lane. This he opened. He then made a careful examination of the sill with his magnifying glass. "Now we shall go upstairs," he said at last.

The banker's dressing room was a plainly furnished little room. It had a gray carpet, a large bureau, and a long mirror. Holmes went to the bureau first, and looked hard at the lock.

"Which key was used to open it?" he asked.

"The one my son mentioned—the key to the cupboard in the lumber room."

"Have you it here?" Holmes asked.

"That is it on the dressing table."

Sherlock picked up the key and opened the bureau.

"It is a noiseless lock," said he. "No wonder it did not wake you. This case, I presume, contains the coronet. We must have a look at it." He opened the leather case. He took out the crown and laid it upon the table. It was a magnificent piece of jewelry. The thirty-six stones were the finest I had ever seen. At one side of the crown was a crooked, cracked edge, where a corner had been torn away.

"Now, Mr. Holder," said Holmes. "Let us try to break off the remaining corner."

The banker looked horrified. "I should not dream of trying," he said.

"Then I will." Holmes suddenly pulled at the coronet with all his strength. Nothing happened. "I feel it give a little," he said. "I am exceptionally strong in the fingers. It would take me quite some time to break it. An ordinary man could not do it. And what do you think would happen if I did break it, Mr. Holder? There would be a noise like a pistol shot. Are you telling me that all this happened within a few yards of your bed—and you heard nothing?"

"I do not know what to think. It is all dark to me," he answered.

"But perhaps it may grow lighter as we go. What do you think, Miss Holder?"

"I confess I share my uncle's confusion," she replied.

"Did your son have on either shoes or slippers when you saw him?"

"He had on nothing except his shirt and trousers."

"Thank you. We have certainly had good luck during this investigation. It will be our own fault if we don't clear the matter up. With your permission, Mr. Holder, I should like to continue my investigation outside."

Holmes went outside alone. He said that any extra

footmarks would make his task more difficult. He was gone an hour or more. When he returned his feet were heavy with snow.

"I think that I have seen all that there is to see, Mr. Holder," said Sherlock Holmes. "I can now serve you best by returning to my rooms in Baker Street."

"But the gems, Mr. Holmes, where are they?"

"I cannot tell," answered Sherlock.

The banker wrung his hands. "I shall never see them again!" he cried. "And my son? Do you give me hope?"

"My opinion is in no way altered," said Sherlock.

"Then for God's sake what happened in my house?" asked the banker.

"Please call on me tomorrow morning between nine and ten at Baker Street. I shall be happy to make things clearer then. I understand that you give me permission to act as I see fit to get the gems back. And I may spend whatever sum necessary to obtain them."

"I would give my fortune to have them back."

"Very good. I shall look into the matter before tomorrow morning. Goodbye, it is just possible that I shall have to return here before this evening."

It was now clear to me that Sherlock Holmes had made up his mind about the case. I could only dimly imagine what conclusions he had come to. Several times during our journey home I tried to get him to tell me. He always changed the subject. At last I gave up in despair. It was not yet three in the afternoon when we arrived at Baker Street. Holmes ran upstairs. In minutes he came down dressed like a bum. His collar was turned up, he wore an old red scarf, his coat was shiny and seedy and his boots were worn.

"I think that this will do," said he, as he looked in the

mirror above the fireplace. "I wish that you could come with me, Watson. But you can't. I may be on the right trail and I may not. But I shall soon find out. I hope to be back in a few hours." He cut a slice of beef from the roast on the sideboard, sandwiched it between two slices of bread, and left.

I had just finished my tea when he returned from his expedition. He was in excellent spirits and swung an old elastic-sided boot in his hand.

He chucked it down into a corner and helped himself to a cup of tea.

"I only looked in as I passed," Holmes said. "I am going right out again."

"Where to?"

"To the other side of town. It may be some time before I get back. Don't wait up in case I should be late."

"How are you getting on with the case?" I asked.

"Oh, so, so. Nothing to complain of. I have been out to the house since I saw you last . . . but I did not go in. It is a very sweet little problem, and I would not have missed it for anything. However, I must not sit here gossiping. I must take these scruffy clothes off and return to my respectable self."

I could see that Sherlock was pleased with himself. There was a twinkle in his eye and there was even a touch of color in his cheeks. He rushed upstairs. A few minutes later I heard the hallway door slam.

I waited until midnight. There was no sign of Holmes, and so I went to bed. Sherlock Holmes sometimes stayed away days and nights on a case, and so I was not alarmed. I do not know what time he returned. When I came down to breakfast there he was. He had a cup of coffee in one hand and a newspaper in the other.

"Please excuse me starting without you, Watson," said he. "But our client has a rather early appointment with me this morning."

"Why, it is after nine now," I answered. "I should not be surprised if that were he. I thought I heard the bell ring."

It was, indeed, our friend the banker. I was shocked by the change in him. His face was now pinched and fallen in and his hair seemed a shade whiter. He seemed weary and sad and dropped into the armchair I pushed forward for him.

"Only two days ago I was a happy man, I hadn't a care in the world," he said. "Now I am both lonely and dishonored. One sorrow comes close on the heels of another. My niece, Mary, has deserted me."

"Deserted you?" Holmes repeated.

"Yes. Her bed has not been slept in. Her room is empty and a note lay on the hall table. Last night I said to her that if she had married my boy all might have turned out well with him. I said it in sorrow, not in anger. Perhaps it was thoughtless of me to say it. She refers to my remark in her note:

MY DEAREST UNCLE—I FEEL THAT I HAVE BROUGHT TROUBLE TO YOU. IF I HAD ACTED DIFFERENTLY, THIS TROUBLE MIGHT NEVER HAVE OCCURRED. KNOWING THIS, I CANNOT BE HAPPY UNDER YOUR ROOF. I FEEL I MUST LEAVE YOU FOREVER. DO NOT WORRY ABOUT MY FUTURE. IT IS PROVIDED FOR.

ABOVE ALL DO NOT SEARCH FOR ME. IN LIFE
OR IN DEATH, I AM ALWAYS YOUR LOVING,
MARY.

What could she mean by that note, Mr. Holmes? Do you
think she means suicide?"

"No, no, nothing of the kind," replied Holmes. "It is
perhaps the best possible solution. I believe, Mr. Holder,
you are nearing the end of your troubles."

"Ha! You say so! You have heard something, Mr.
Holmes! You have learned something! Where are the
gems?"

"Would you think a thousand pounds apiece too much
to pay for their return?"

"I would pay ten."

"That would be unnecessary. Three thousand will
cover the matter. And I believe you have offered a reward.
Have you your checkbook? Better make it out for four
thousand pounds."

The banker made out the check. Holmes walked over
to his desk and took out a little triangular piece of gold.
Three gems shined out from it. He threw it on the table.

The banker picked it up with a shriek of joy.

"You have it!" he gasped. "I am saved! I am saved!"

"There is one other thing you owe, Mr. Holder," said
Sherlock Holmes rather sternly.

"Owe?" He picked up his pen. "Name the sum and I
will pay."

"No, the debt is not to me. You owe a very humble
apology to that noble lad, your son. Were he my son, I
should be proud of the way he handled himself throughout
this matter."

"Then it was not Arthur who took them?" asked the banker.

"I told you yesterday, and I repeat it today. It was not."

"You are sure of it! Then let us hurry to him at once. He should know that the truth is out."

"He knows it already. After I cleared up the case, I had an interview with him. He would not tell me the story, and so I told him. He had to admit I was right. He even added the very few details which were not clear to me."

"For heaven's sake, tell me, what is this extraordinary mystery."

"I will do so, and I will show you the steps by which I reached it. Let me say the worst first. Sir George Burnwell and your niece Mary have fled together!"

"My Mary? Impossible!" cried Holder.

"It is more than possible," replied Holmes. "It is certain. Neither you nor your son knew the true character of this man. He is one of the most dangerous men in England! He is a ruined gambler, an absolutely desperate villain. He is a man without heart or conscience. Your niece knew nothing of such men. When he courted her, she believed she alone had touched his heart. The devil only knows what he told her. Whatever it was, she became his tool. She saw him nearly every evening."

"I cannot, and I will not believe it!" cried the banker.

"I will tell you what happened in your house the other night. When your niece thought you were in bed, she slipped downstairs. She spoke with her lover through the hall window overlooking the stable lane. He stood there so long that his footprints were pressed right through the snow. She told him of the coronet. He convinced her that they must steal it. She had just heard his instructions, when she saw you coming downstairs. She closed the window quickly. To divert your attention she told you about the maid and her wooden-legged lover.

"Arthur went to bed after asking you to lend him money. He slept badly because of his worry over his club debts. In the middle of the night he heard footsteps pass by his door. He rose and was surprised to see his cousin tiptoeing along the passage. She disappeared into your dressing room. He was astonished at the sight. He slipped on some clothes and waited in the dark to see what would happen next. Presently, she emerged from the room. She carried the precious coronet in her hands. He hid behind a curtain and watched in horror as she walked downstairs and opened the hall window. He saw her hand the coronet to someone outside, close the window once more and hurry back to her room.

"His love for her stopped him from acting. But the instant she was gone he came to his senses. He realized how crushed you would be by the theft. He knew he had to set it right. He rushed down in his bare feet. He opened the window and sprang out into the snow. He then ran down the lane. He could see a dark figure in the moonlight. It was Sir George Burnwell. He tried to get away but Arthur caught him. A struggle began between them. Each tugged at the coronet. Your son struck Sir George and cut him over the eye. Then something suddenly snapped. Finding the coronet in his hands, Arthur rushed back to the house. He closed the window and went up to your room. Only then did he notice that the coronet was twisted. He was trying to straighten it when you saw him."

"Is it possible?" gasped the banker.

"You then roused his anger by calling him names

—right when he felt he deserved your warmest thanks. He could not explain the true state of affairs without betraying the woman he loved."

"And that was why she shrieked when she saw the coronet. She thought Burnwell had it!" cried Holder. "My God! What a blind fool I have been. And his asking to go out for five minutes! The dear fellow wanted to see if he could find the missing piece. How cruelly I misjudged him!"

"When I arrived at the house," continued Sherlock Holmes, "I at once looked over the snow. I knew none had fallen since the evening before. The impressions, therefore, would help me in my investigation. I passed along the tradesmen's path. It was all trampled down and the tracks were impossible to make out. Near the kitchen door, however, I could see the prints of a woman. She had talked to a man with a wooden leg. This I could tell by the round impression it had made in the snow. I could even see that someone had disturbed them. Her deep toe and light heel marks showed that she had run back to the door. Wooden-leg had waited a little and then gone away. You had already told me about the maid and her admirers. And so I assumed the tracks belonged to her and a sweetheart. Inquiry showed I was right. I passed around the garden and saw a few tracks. These I believed were made by the police. When I got to the stable lane I found what I was looking for. A very long and complex story was written in the snow.

"There was a double line of tracks made by a booted man. There was also a double line of tracks made by barefeet. I was convinced that these were made by your son, Arthur. The booted man had walked, while the barefoot man had run swiftly. In spots the barefoot prints rubbed out the booted ones. I therefore knew that the barefoot man had come after the booted man. I followed the tracks. They led to the hall window. The snow was worn where Boots had waited for some time. Then I walked to the other end of the lane. I saw that Boots had turned around. I also saw where the snow had been cut up by a struggle. And I noticed a few drops of blood. Boots had then run down the lane. Another smudge of blood showed that it was he who was hurt. His tracks led directly to the high road. The pavement had been cleared and so there were no further clues.

"I then went back to the house. I examined the hall window with my magnifying glass. I could see that someone had passed out. I could also see a wet print where someone had come in again. I was beginning to form an opinion as to what had happened. A man had waited outside the window and someone had brought him the gems. The deed had been seen by your son. He had pursued the thief and had struggled with him. Their united strength had torn the coronet. He had returned with the prize, but had left a fragment in the thief's grasp. The question now was: Who was the man and who brought him the coronet?

"It is my belief that when you have excluded the impossible, you are left with the truth. I knew that you could not have brought the coronet to the window. That left your niece and the maids. But if Lucy Parr or one of the other maids had done it, why would your son shield them? There could be no possible reason. But you said that he loved his cousin Mary and had wanted to marry her. This was an excellent reason why he should want to protect her.

I remembered how you had seen her at the hall window and how she had fainted on seeing the coronet. I knew then that I was right.

"And to whom could she have given the crown? It had to be to a lover. Only his love would outweigh her love for you. I knew you went out little and that your circle of friends was a small one. But among them was Sir George Burnwell. I had heard before that he had a reputation of being a ladies' man. It must have been he who wore those boots and now had the gems. I guessed Sir George would feel pretty safe. He knew Arthur was unlikely to say anything against his own cousin.

"Well, your own good sense will tell you what I did next. I dressed up like a bum and went to Sir George's house. I managed to talk with his valet. I found out that Sir George had cut his head the night before. I then bought a pair of his old shoes from the valet. These I took to your house. They matched the tracks in the snow exactly."

"I saw a bum in the lane yesterday," said Mr. Holder.

"Precisely. It was I. I found that I had my man and so I went home and changed. I knew that I would have to be careful in dealing with Sir George. He was smart enough to know we could not bring him to trial. The scandal would be too great. And so I went to see him. At first he denied the theft. But I told him point by point everything that had happened. He had no defense. Angrily, he picked up a cane to strike me. But I knew my man! I put a pistol to his head before he could strike. Then he became a little more reasonable. I told him that we would give him a price for the stones—a thousand pounds apiece.

" 'Why dash it all!' said he. 'I've sold all three for six hundred pounds!' I promised him that the police would not be involved and soon managed to get the address of the man who bought them. I soon found that man. After some bargaining I got the stones back for a thousand apiece. Then I looked in on your son and told him that all was right. I got to bed at two o'clock after what I may call a really hard day's work."

"Sir," said the banker, rising, "you will not find me ungrateful. As to what you tell me about poor Mary, it breaks my heart. Can you tell me where she now is?"

"I think we can safely say that she is wherever Sir George Burnwell is. And in his company, she is bound to receive her own punishment for her wrongdoings."

"It is a sad situation indeed. I must go now to my dear boy and apologize for the wrong which I have done him. Mr. Holmes, your skill has exceeded all I have heard of it. You have single-handedly saved England from a great scandal! I cannot find the words to thank you."

The
Adventure
of
Silver
Blaze

Conan Doyle did not list this tale as one of his "best" but it is considered by many to be one of his masterpieces. The reason for this is only too clear—the story is intriguing and highly original. Holmes is in top form and the use of a horse as the central figure in a mystery is most unusual.

Toward the end of the first twelve adventures written by Conan Doyle for the *Strand* magazine, he thought of slaying Sherlock Holmes. "He takes my mind from better things," Conan Doyle complained. But his editors would have none of it. They knew that Holmes had become the favorite hero of millions of readers throughout the world. And they knew that there would be a public uproar if Conan Doyle killed him off. So they urged Conan Doyle for more adventures. Finally he bowed to public demand and wrote twelve more. In December 1892 the first new adventure appeared in the *Strand* magazine. It was *The Adventure of Silver Blaze.*

The Adventure
of Silver Blaze

"I am afraid, Watson, that I shall have to go," said
Sherlock Holmes. We had just sat down to breakfast in his
rooms at Number 221B Baker Street.

"Go!" said I. "Where to?"

"To Dartmoor—to King's Pyland Stable."

I was not surprised. In fact, I had wondered why he
was not already involved in this extraordinary case. News
of it had been in the papers for days and it was the topic of
conversation all over England. Silver Blaze was the favorite
horse to run in the Wessex Cup race. He had disappeared
and his trainer had been murdered. It was just the type of
strange mystery Sherlock Holmes liked best.

"If I won't be in the way, I'd very much like to go down
with you," I commented.

"My dear Watson," said Holmes, "you would be doing
me a great favor by coming. And I believe your time will be
well-spent. There are many points about the case which
make it absolutely unique. We have just time to catch the
train for Dartmoor. I'll tell you more about it on board."

An hour or so later we were in the corner of a first-
class carriage, flying along toward a new adventure.
Holmes sat across from me, his sharp, eager face framed by
his earflapped traveling cap.

"I presume you have already read about the murder of
John Straker and the disappearance of Silver Blaze?" he
said.

"I have seen what *The Telegraph* and *The Chronicle* have to say," I answered.

"The problem is that everyone has had a word to say on the subject. It is difficult to sift fact from fiction. But that is exactly what we must do. On Tuesday evening I received two telegraphs. One was from Colonel Ross, the owner of the horse. The other was from Inspector Gregory, who is in charge of the case. Both wanted my assistance."

"Tuesday evening!" I exclaimed. "And this is Thursday morning. Why didn't you go down yesterday?"

"Because I made a blunder—yes, even I can make a mistake, Watson. The fact is that I thought it not possible for the most remarkable horse in England to remain missing for long. I felt sure the horse—and the murderer of John Straker—would turn up. And so I waited, expecting to hear of some new development at any moment. But when the only news that came was of Fitzroy Simpson's arrest, and an entire day had passed, well, I knew that it was time for me to take action. Still, I don't believe yesterday was wasted."

"You have a theory then?" I asked eagerly.

"Well, I believe I understand the basic facts of the case. I shall tell you what I know. Nothing clears up a case better than explaining it to another person. Besides, you shall have to know the details if you are to be of any assistance."

I lay back waiting to hear his story. Holmes leaned forward. As he spoke, his long, thin forefinger checked off the points of the case upon the palm of his left hand.

"Silver Blaze," he said, "is from a long line of thoroughbred racehorses. He is now in his fifth year and has won race after race. He is the favorite to win in all his races. The public likes to place bets on him with the bookmakers, or bookies, as they are called, even though as the favorite he pays off little. As is the way with all betting, the greater the odds against something winning, the more it pays off if it in fact wins. Therefore if one bets on the favorite and he should win, one only profits slightly. On the other hand, if one bets on a longshot, and he wins, that pays off well. One can win back one's money a hundred times over! The bookies like to know ahead of time who is actually going to win. In that way they don't take bets that will end up costing them a fortune. Now, there are many people who would prefer the favorite not to run, so that their own horse will have a better chance at winning.

"Of course, Silver Blaze's owner, Colonel Ross, understood all this. He has a stable called King's Pyland. It is a small training stable that only owns four horses. Ross did everything possible to guard the favorite. His trainer was an ex-jockey named John Straker. Straker wore the stable's colors of black and red for five years. But he became too heavy to ride as a jockey and so became a trainer. Both as a jockey and as a trainer he was a loyal and honest employee. Three stableboys worked under Straker. One of these lads sat up each night in the stable, while the others slept in the hayloft. All three came to Ross with excellent references. John Straker was a married man and lived in a small house two hundred yards from the stable. He had no children, kept one maid servant and was comfortably off. The area around the house is lonely. There is a small cluster of cottages about a half-mile to the north. These are for the use of invalids and others who may wish to enjoy the pure Dartmoor air. The village of Tavistock lies two miles to the west. Also about two miles away—across the moor—is another training stable. It is called Mapleton, belongs to Lord Backwater and is managed by a Mr. Silas Brown. In every other direction the moor is complete wilderness.

"Now, on Monday evening the horses at King's Pyland were exercised and watered as usual. The stable was locked at nine o'clock. Two of the lads walked up to the trainer's house for supper. The third lad, named Ned Hunter, remained on guard. A few minutes after nine, the maid, Edith Baxter, carried Ned's supper down to the stable. It was a dish of curried lamb. The maid also carried a lantern as it was very dark and she had to walk across the open moor.

"Edith Baxter was within thirty yards of the stable when a man appeared out of the darkness. He called to her to stop. As he stepped into the light cast from the lantern, she saw him. He looked like a gentleman. He was dressed in a gray tweed suit, wore a cloth cap, and had a red scarf tied about his neck. She noticed that he carried a heavy walking stick with a knob at its end. She was particularly struck by the paleness of his face and by his extremely nervous manner.

" 'Can you tell me where I am?' he asked. 'I thought I was going to have to sleep on the moor until I saw your light.'

" 'You are close to the King's Pyland training stable,' she said.

" 'Indeed! What a stroke of luck!' he cried. 'I understand that a stableboy sleeps there alone every night. Perhaps that is his supper which you are carrying to him now. . . . How would you like to earn the price of a new dress?' he said. He took a piece of paper from his pocket. 'See that the boy is given this tonight and you shall have the prettiest dress money can buy.'

"The girl was frightened by the stranger's manner. She ran past him to the little window where she always handed the lad his meals. It was already open. She had just begun to tell Ned what had happened, when the stranger came up again.

" 'Good evening,' said he and looked through the window at the stableboy. 'I wanted to have a word with you.' The girl has since sworn that as he spoke she noticed a corner of the paper sticking out from his closed hand.

" 'What business have you here?' asked the lad.

" 'It's business that could put some money in your pocket,' said the man. 'You've two horses running in the Wessex Cup—Silver Blaze and Bayard. Tell me the truth and you'll do all right for yourself. Is it true that the stable has bet on Bayard and plans to let him win the race?'

" 'So you're one of those damned bookies!' cried the lad. 'I'll show you how we treat your kind here at King's Pyland.' He sprang up and rushed across the stable to untie the dog. Meanwhile, the girl fled to the house. As she ran she glanced back. The stranger was leaning through the window. A minute later Hunter rushed out of the stable with the dog. He ran all around the buildings, but the man was gone."

"One moment!" I interrupted. "Did the stableboy leave the door unlocked when he ran out with the dog?"

"Excellent, Watson, excellent!" exclaimed Sherlock Holmes. "I was struck by that same thought. In fact, I wired Dartmoor yesterday to find out. The boy locked the door behind him when he left the stable. The window, I may add, was not large enough for a man to get through.

"Hunter waited until the other stableboys had returned. Then he sent a message to the trainer telling him what had happened. Straker appeared very upset by the incident. Later that night, he and his wife went to bed. At about one o'clock Mrs. Straker was awakened by sounds in their room. It was her husband dressing. He told her that he was worried about the horses and could not sleep. He said that he was going to walk down to the stable and make sure all was well. It had begun to rain out and Mrs. Straker begged her husband to stay indoors. But he did not listen. He put on his raincoat and went out.

"In the morning Mrs. Straker awoke to find her husband had not returned. She dressed quickly, called the maid, and set off for the stable. The door was open. She found Hunter huddled in a chair. Silver Blaze was gone and there was no sign of his trainer.

"The two boys who slept in the hayloft were quickly awakened. No sense could be got out of Hunter. He had obviously been drugged. They left him to sleep it off and went out in search of horse and trainer. They climbed to the hill near the house from where they had a good view of the neighboring moors. There were no signs of the horse ... but they could see something else.

"About a quarter of a mile from the stable John Straker's overcoat was flapping upon a bush. They rushed over to it. Right near the overcoat was a little pit or hollow in the earth. At the bottom of it they found John Straker. He was dead. His head had been shattered by the savage blow of a heavy weapon. He was also wounded in the thigh by what looked like a sharp instrument. It was clear that he had defended himself against his attackers. In his right hand was a small knife. It was clotted with blood. In his left hand he held a red silk scarf. The maid immediately recognized it. It had been worn by the stranger who had visited the stable the night before.

"When Hunter recovered, he, too, was positive that the scarf had belonged to the stranger. He was equally certain that the stranger had slipped something into his supper while standing at the window.

"As to the missing horse—the tracks in the mud showed that he had been at the scene of the struggle. But from that morning to this he has not been seen. A large reward has been offered, but there has been no news of him. The stableboy's dinner was found to contain opium. The people in the house ate the same meal, but no traces of the drug were found in its remains.

"Those are the main facts of the case. I shall now tell you what the police have done so far.

"Inspector Gregory is an extremely good officer. On his arrival he promptly found and arrested the stranger. There was little difficulty in finding him as he has been living in one of those nearby cottages. His name is Fitzroy Simpson. It seems that he comes from a well-off family and has had an excellent education. But as a young man he gambled away his money. He now lives by taking bets. An examination of his betting book showed that he bet heavily against the favorite in next week's race. This means, of course, that he had a strong motive in preventing Silver Blaze from running that race.

"When Simpson was arrested, he was asked his version of the incident. He claimed that he came down to

Dartmoor for first-hand information on Silver Blaze, Bayard, and Mapleton's horse, Desborough. He did not deny what had happened at the stable. But he insisted that he was there simply to gain information about the horses. When the Inspector showed him the scarf, Simpson turned white. He could not account for its presence in the hand of the murdered man. His wet clothing proved that he had been out in the storm. His stick was weighted with lead and was just the type of weapon that could have killed the trainer. The evidence certainly pointed to him.

"On the other hand, there was no wound on his body. Yet, Straker's knife was covered in blood. This fact, then, was Simpson's one defense. There you have it in a nutshell, Watson. If you can shed any light on the matter I would be most obliged."

I had listened with great interest to Holmes' story. "Is it possible," I said, "that the cut wound was caused by Straker himself. His brain injury would have caused his whole body to convulse—to shudder uncontrollably. He could have fallen on the knife and cut himself."

"It is more than possible, it is most likely," said Holmes. "But if the blood on the knife is Straker's rather than an attacker's, Simpson could be that attacker after all. Take away the need for a wounded attacker, and you take away Simpson's only defense."

"Well, even after you explain everything to me, I still do not understand how the police put the pieces of the puzzle together," I said.

"From what I understand, the police's theory is this: Fitzroy Simpson drugged the lad with the powdered opium. He somehow had a duplicate key to the stable door which he used to let himself in. The horse's bridle is missing. Therefore, Simpson must have put this on the horse and then led him out of the stable to kidnap him. He left the door open behind him and led the horse away over the moor. Suddenly he either met or was overtaken by the trainer. A fight naturally followed. Simpson beat the trainer's head with his heavy stick. He, himself, managed to escape injury from Straker's knife. Then the thief either led the horse to some secret hiding place, or the horse bolted and is now wandering over the moors. That is the case as it appears to the police. It seems unlikely, but until we arrive at the scene of the crime, it is all the explanation we have."

It was evening before we reached the little town of Tavistock. Two gentlemen were waiting for us at the station. One was a tall, fair man with lionlike hair and beard and light blue eyes. The other was a small, alert person dressed very neatly, with trim little side-whiskers and an eye-glass. The tall man was Colonel Ross and the other was Inspector Gregory.

"I am delighted that you have come down, Mr. Holmes," said the Colonel. "The Inspector here has done all that could possibly be suggested. However, I wish to leave no stone unturned in finding my horse and avenging poor Straker's death."

"Have there been any fresh developments?" asked Holmes.

"I am sorry to say that we have made very little progress," said the Inspector. "We have an open carriage outside. I am sure you will want to see the stable before it grows dark. We can talk as we drive."

A minute later we were all seated in a comfortable carriage, rattling through the quaint English town. Inspector Gregory spoke at length about the case. Every once in a while Holmes asked a question or made a comment. Colonel Ross leaned back with his arms folded and his hat tilted over his eyes while I listened with interest to the dialogue of the two detectives.

"The net is drawn pretty close around Fitzroy Simpson," Gregory said, "and I believe he is our man. At the same time I realize that some new development may come along to upset the theory."

"How about Straker's knife?" Holmes asked.

"We have come to the conclusion that he wounded himself in the fall."

"My friend, Doctor Watson, made that same suggestion to me in the train. If that is true, then this man Simpson could be the murderer after all."

"Undoubtedly. He had a great interest in the disappearance of the favorite. He could have drugged the stableboy. We know that he was out in the storm, he was armed with a heavy stick, and his scarf was found in the dead man's hand. I really think we have enough evidence to go before a jury."

Holmes shook his head. "A clever lawyer would tear it to shreds," he said. "Why should he take the horse out of the stable? If he wished to injure it, why couldn't he do it there? Has a duplicate key been found on him? What chemist sold him the powdered opium? Above all, where could he—a stranger in the district—hide a horse, especially so famous a horse? What is his own explanation of the paper which he wished to give the maid and the stableboy?"

"He says it was a ten-pound note. One was found in his purse. But your other questions are not so difficult to answer. He is not a stranger in the district. He has spent two summers in Tavistock. The opium was probably bought in London. The key could have been thrown away. The horse may lie at the bottom of one of the pits or old mines upon the moor."

"And what does he say about his scarf?"

"He admits that it is his. He says he lost it. And a new clue may answer your question about why he led the horse away from the stable."

Holmes pricked up his ears.

"We have found traces which show that a party of gypsies camped within a mile of the spot where the murder took place on Monday night. On Tuesday they were gone. There could have been some understanding between Simpson and those gypsies. He could have been leading the horse to them, when Straker came upon him. The gypsies could have the horse now."

"It is certainly possible," said Holmes.

"The moor is being searched thoroughly for any sign of the gypsies. I have also examined every stable and outhouse in and around Tavistock."

"I understand there is another training stable nearby," Holmes said.

"Yes, and that is a fact we have not neglected. Their horse, Desborough, is the second favorite in the race next week. It would certainly be to their advantage for Silver Blaze not to race. Silas Brown, the trainer, is known to have bet on the race and he was no friend of Straker. We have, however, examined the stable and there is nothing to connect him to the affair."

"And nothing to connect this man Simpson to the Mapleton Stable?" Holmes asked.

"Nothing at all."

Holmes leaned back in the carriage and the conversation stopped. A few minutes later our driver pulled up at King's Pyland. A neat little red brick house stood at the side of the road. Some distance off was a long gray-tiled outbuilding. In every other direction were the curving moors, and in the distance a cluster of houses, which belonged to Mapleton Stable. We all jumped out of the carriage. All except Holmes, that is, who seemed lost in thought. I touched him on the arm. He gave a violent start and stepped out of the carriage.

"Excuse me," he said. "I was daydreaming." There was a gleam in his eyes and some form of excitement in his manner. I was used to Sherlock Holmes' ways. Something told me that his hand was upon a clue. What it was, however, I could not imagine.

"Perhaps you would like to go at once to the scene of the crime, Mr. Holmes?" asked Gregory.

"I think I should prefer to stay here a while. I would like to go into one or two questions in detail. Straker was brought here, I presume?"

"Yes, he lies upstairs," Gregory answered.

"He has worked for you for some years, Colonel Ross?"

"I have always found him an excellent employee."

"Did you make an inventory of what was in his pockets at the time of his death, Inspector?"

"I have the things themselves in the sitting room if you should care to see them."

"I should like to," Sherlock Holmes answered.

We all filed into the front room and sat around the

central table. The Inspector unlocked a square tin box and laid a heap of things before us. There was a box of matches, a piece of candle, a pipe, a pouch of tobacco, a silver watch with a gold chain, five coins, an aluminum pencil case, a few papers, and an ivory-handled knife with a very delicate but strong blade marked Weiss & Co., London.

"This is a very unique knife," said Holmes. He lifted it up and examined it carefully. "Since I see bloodstains on it, I assume this is the knife which was found in the dead man's hand. Watson, this knife is surely in your line."

"It is used in very delicate medical operations."

"I thought so. A very delicate blade devised for very delicate work. A strange thing for a man to carry with him on a walk . . . especially since it does not shut."

"The tip was guarded by a disc of cork which we found beside the body," said the Inspector. "His wife tells us that the knife has lain on the dressing table for some days. He picked it up as he left the room. It was a poor weapon, but perhaps the best that he could lay his hand on at that moment."

"Very possibly. How about these papers?" asked Holmes.

"Three of them are receipts for hay. One of them is a letter of instructions from Colonel Ross. This other is from a dressmaker named Madame Lesurier of Bond Street, London. It is a bill and is addressed to a William Darbyshire. Mrs. Straker tells us that Darbyshire was a friend of her husband's. Letters were sometimes sent to him here."

"Madame Darbyshire had somewhat expensive tastes," remarked Holmes as he glanced at the bill. "The dress described cost twenty pounds! Well, there appears to be nothing more to learn here. We may now go down to the scene of the crime."

As we left the front room, a woman stepped forward and put her hand on the Inspector's sleeve. Her face was worn and thin and eager. It was stamped with the print of recent horror.

"Have you got them? Have you found them?" she asked.

"No, Mrs. Straker. But Mr. Holmes here has come from London to help us. We shall do all that is possible."

"Surely I met you at Plymouth at a garden party some time ago, Mrs. Straker," said Holmes.

"No, sir, you are mistaken."

"Dear me, why I could have sworn to it. You wore a costume of dove-colored silk with ostrich feather trimming."

"I never had such a dress, sir," answered the lady.

"Ah, that settles it," said Holmes. With an apology, he followed the Inspector outside. A short walk across the moor took us to where the body was found. The bush where the coat had hung was nearby.

"There was no wind that night, I understand," said Holmes.

"None, but very heavy rain."

"In that case the overcoat was not blown against the bushes. It was placed there."

"Yes, it was laid across the bush," answered the Inspector.

"You fill me with interest," said Holmes. "I see that the ground has been trampled down a good deal. No doubt many feet have been here since Monday night."

"A piece of matting has been laid here at the side. We have all stood on that."

"Excellent," exclaimed Holmes.

The Inspector held out a bag which he had been carrying. "In this bag I have one of the boots which Straker wore, one of Fitzroy Simpson's shoes, and a cast horseshoe of Silver Blaze."

"My dear Inspector," exclaimed Sherlock Holmes. "You surpass yourself!" Holmes took the bag and walked closer to the hollow where the body was found. He shifted the mat into a more central position. Then he lay face-down on the mat, leaning his chin up on his hands. In this position, he made a careful study of the trampled mud.

"Hallo!" said he suddenly. "What's this?"

It was a half-burned stick match. It was so coated with mud that it looked at first like a little chip of wood.

"I cannot see how I overlooked it," said the Inspector.

"It was invisible because it was buried in the mud. I only saw it because I was looking for it," said Holmes.

"What! You expected to find it?" exclaimed the Inspector.

"I thought it not unlikely." He took the boxes from the bag and compared the impressions of each shoe with the marks on the ground. Then he climbed up to the rim of the hollow and crawled about among the ferns and bushes.

"I am afraid there are no more tracks," said the Inspector. "I have examined the ground very carefully for a hundred yards in each direction."

"Indeed!" said Holmes, rising. "Then I will not do it again. But I should like to take a little walk over the moor before it grows dark. I think I shall put this horseshoe into my pocket for luck."

Colonel Ross looked impatiently at his watch.

"I wish you would come back with me, Inspector," said Ross. "I would like your advice on several points. I especially want to know whether we owe it to the public to withdraw our horse from the race."

"Certainly not!" cried Holmes. "Keep the horse entered in the race."

The Colonel bowed. "I am very glad to have had your opinion, sir," said he. "You will find us at poor Straker's house when you have finished your walk. We can drive back to Tavistock together."

He and the Inspector started down the hill, while Holmes and I slowly walked across the moor. For a long while Holmes walked in silence, sunk in the deepest thought.

"It's this way, Watson," he said at last. "Let us not talk of who killed John Straker for a moment. Let us deal only with finding out what has become of the horse. Now, suppose he broke away after or during the tragedy. Where could he have gone to? If left to himself, he surely would have run back to King's Pyland or else to Mapleton Stable. Why should he run wildly over the moors? He would have been seen by now. And why should the gypsies kidnap him? These people always clear out when they hear of trouble. They do not want to be pestered by the police. They could not hope to sell such a horse. He is too easily recognized. They would run the great risk of being caught and accused of theft, and they would gain nothing at all. Surely that is clear."

"Where is he, then?" I asked.

"I have already said that he must have gone to King's

Pyland or to Mapleton. He is not at King's Pyland, therefore he is at Mapleton. Let us assume that this is fact for a moment and see where it leads us. This part of the moor is very hard and dry. You can see from here that there is a long hollow over yonder. That area must have been wet Monday night. If he traveled to Mapleton then he must have crossed the hollow. That is where we must go to look for tracks."

We walked briskly over to the hollow. Holmes walked down the bank to the left and I to the right in search of the horse's tracks. I had not gone fifty paces when I heard Holmes shout and saw him wave to me. The track of a horse was plainly outlined in the soft earth in front of him. He took the horseshoe from his pocket. It fit exactly.

"See the value of imagination," said Holmes. "We imagined what might have happened, acted on our theory, and were rewarded for it. Let us proceed."

We crossed the marshy land and passed over a quarter mile of dry, hard turf. Again the ground sloped, and again we came on the tracks. Then we lost them for half a mile, only to pick them up again quite close to Mapleton. However, something had changed. There were now a man's tracks besides those of the horse's.

"The horse was alone before!" I cried.

"Quite so. Hallo, what is this?"

The double track turned sharply off in the direction of King's Pyland. Holmes whistled and we both followed after it. His eyes were on the trail, but I happened to look a little to one side. To my surprise I saw the same tracks coming back again in the opposite direction.

"One for you, Watson!" said Holmes. "The horse and

man must have turned about at some point. You have saved us a long walk—one which would have brought us right back here. Let us follow the return track."

We had not to go far. It ended at the asphalt path which led to the gates of Mapleton Stable. As we approached a groom ran out.

"We don't want anyone hanging about here," he said.

"I only wish to ask one question," said Holmes. "If I were to call on Silas Brown at five o'clock tomorrow morning, would he be up?"

"Bless you, sir. If anyone is about it will be he. He is always the first one up. But here he is, sir. He can answer your questions himself." Holmes took out a coin with which to tip the boy.

"No, sir, no. I'd lose my job if he saw me taking your money. Afterward, if you like."

Holmes had just put the coin back in his pocket when a fierce-looking man walked up. He strode out from the gate with a whip swinging in his hand.

"What's this, Dawson?" he cried. "No gossiping! Go about your business! And you—what the devil do you want here?"

"Ten minutes talk with you, my good sir," said Holmes in the sweetest of voices.

"I've no time to talk to every wanderer. We want no strangers here. Be off, or you may find a dog at your heels."

Holmes leaned forward and whispered something in the trainer's ear.

"It's a lie!" he shouted. "An infernal lie!"

"Very good! Shall we argue about it here in public, or talk about it in your parlor?" asked Holmes.

"Oh, come in if you wish."

Holmes smiled. "I shall not keep you more than a few minutes, Watson," he said.

It was nearly twenty minutes, however, before Holmes and the trainer returned. Silas Brown's manner had completely changed. His face was ashly pale and beads of sweat shone on his brow. His hands shook so much that his whip nearly fell out of them.

"Your instructions will be done," he told Holmes meekly.

"There must be no mistake," said Holmes.

"Oh, no, there shall be no mistake. It shall be there. Should I change it first or not?"

Holmes thought a little and then burst out laughing. "No, don't," said he. "I shall write to you about it. No tricks now or—"

"Oh, you can trust me. You can trust me!" said the trainer.

"Yes, I think I can. Well, you shall hear from me tomorrow." The man held out a trembling hand to Holmes, but Holmes did not shake it. Instead, he turned on his heel and we set off for King's Pyland.

"Master Silas Brown is the perfect combination of bully, coward, and sneak," remarked Holmes as we trudged along together.

"He has the horse then?" I asked.

"He tried to get out of it. But I described to him all the events which took place that morning. He was convinced that I had been watching him the whole time! His boots matched the tracks exactly. Besides, no employee of his would have dared to do such a thing. I described to him that he was the first down in the morning, that he saw a strange horse wandering over the moor—and went out to it. I told him that he was astonished to see the silvery-white forehead which belongs to Silver Blaze. He had in his power the only horse which could beat his own. Without it in the race, he stood to win a great deal of money on his horse. Then I described to him that he first had thought of leading Silver Blaze back to King's Pyland. But on second thought he had decided to keep the horse and hide him at Mapleton until the race was run. When I told him every detail, he was speechless. He wished only to save his own skin."

"But his stables had been searched."

"Oh, an old horse-faker like he knows many tricks," said Sherlock Holmes.

"But aren't you afraid to leave the horse in his care? He has every interest in injuring him," I commented.

"My dear fellow, he will guard it with his life. He knows that his only hope of mercy is to produce the horse."

"Even if he does produce the horse, Colonel Ross did not seem like a man who will show him much mercy."

"The matter does not rest with Colonel Ross. I follow my own methods. I can tell as much or as little as I choose. That is the advantage of being unofficial. I don't know if you noticed it, Watson, but the Colonel seemed a bit annoyed by me and my methods. I think I shall now have some fun at his expense. Say nothing to him about the horse."

"Certainly not without your permission," said I.

"But of course, all this is quite a minor point compared to the question of who killed John Straker."

"And you will now work on that?"

"On the contrary, we both go back to London by the night train."

I was thunderstruck by my friend's words. We had only been in the country a few hours. I could not understand why he should give up an investigation now just when he had begun it so brilliantly. But he would say no more until we were at the trainer's house. The Colonel and the Inspector were waiting for us in the parlor.

"My friend and I return to town by the midnight express," said Holmes. "We have had a charming little breath of your Dartmoor air."

The Inspector opened his eyes, and the Colonel's lip curled up in a sneer.

"So you cannot find the murderer of poor Straker?" said the Colonel.

Holmes shrugged his shoulders. "There are certainly some serious difficulties in the way. I have every hope, however, that your horse will race on Tuesday. I beg you to have your jockey prepared. Might I ask for a photograph of Mr. John Straker?"

The Inspector took one from an envelope in his pocket and handed it to Holmes.

"My dear Gregory, you really outdo yourself! Please wait here an instant. I have a question I wish to ask the maid."

"I must say that I am rather disappointed in our London consultant," said Colonel Ross as soon as Holmes had left the room. "I do not see that we are any further along in the case than when he came."

"At least, you have his word that your horse will run on Tuesday," I said.

"Yes. I have his word. But I would rather have the horse," commented Colonel Ross.

I was about to defend my friend when Holmes entered the room again.

"Now, gentlemen," he said. "I am quite ready to leave for Tavistock."

We walked outside. A carriage was waiting. A stableboy held the door open for us. Holmes tapped the boy on the shoulder.

"You have a few sheep in the paddock, I see," Holmes commented. "Who takes care of them?"

"I do, sir."

"Have you noticed any change in them lately?"

"Well, sir, not really—'cept three of them have gone lame."

I could see that Holmes was very pleased with the boy's answer. He chuckled and rubbed his hands together.

"A long shot, Watson, a very long shot!" he said, pinching my arm. "Gregory, if I were you I'd pay some attention to these sheep. Drive on, coachman!"

Colonel Ross still seemed annoyed at Holmes. Inspector Gregory, however, was very much interested in what my friend had to say.

"You consider the sheep going lame of importance?" he asked.

"Exceedingly so," answered Sherlock Holmes.

"Is there any other point you feel is important?"

"Yes. Also of importance is the curious incident of the dog on the night of the murder."

"The dog did nothing in particular that night," said Gregory.

"That was the curious incident," remarked Sherlock Holmes.

Four days later Holmes and I were again on the train bound for Dartmoor. This time we were on our way to see the Wessex Cup race. Colonel Ross met us at the station and together we drove to the track. His face was grave and his manner was extremely cold toward us.

"I have seen nothing of my horse," said he.

"I suppose you would know him if you saw him?" asked Holmes.

The Colonel glared at Holmes angrily. "I have been working with racehorses for twenty years. No one has ever asked me such a question. A child would know Silver Blaze. His markings are distinct. He has a white forehead and spotted foreleg."

"How is the betting?" Holmes asked.

We looked up at where the bets were posted. Silver Blaze was the favorite!

"Hum!" said Holmes. "Somebody knows something, that is clear."

Just then the horses began to line up at the gate. Overhead we heard the horses and their riders being announced. Silver Blaze was included.

"All six horses to race have been mentioned," exclaimed Colonel Ross. "But I don't see my horse!"

"Only five have lined up," I said. "This must be he."

As I spoke a powerful bay horse cantered past us. The Colonel's jockey was astride him, wearing King's Pyland's colors of black and red.

"That's my rider and my colors but that is not my horse!" cried the owner. "That beast hasn't a white hair on his whole body. What is going on, Holmes?"

"Well, well, let us see how the horse runs," said my

friend, calmly. For a few minutes he gazed through my binoculars. "Capital! An excellent start!" he cried suddenly. "There they are, coming around the curve now!"

We had a superb view of the horses as they came around the stretch. The six horses were running closely together. Just before they reached us, Desborough of Mapleton Stable took the lead. But not for long. The horse wearing the Colonel's colors suddenly overtook Desborough. He rushed forward and won by six lengths.

"Well, I've won the race, anyway," gasped the Colonel. "But I confess I can make neither head nor tail out of it. Don't you think you have kept up your mystery long enough, Mr. Holmes?"

"Certainly, Colonel. You shall know everything. Let us go around and have a look at the horse together. Here he is," he continued as we made our way to the winner's circle. "You have only to wash his face and his leg to find that he is the same old Silver Blaze as ever."

"You take my breath away!" exclaimed the Colonel.

"I found him in the hands of a faker and decided to run him just as he was sent over," explained Sherlock Holmes.

"My dear sir, you have done wonders. The horse looks very fit and well. It never raced better in its life. I owe you a thousand apologies for having doubted your ability. You have done me a great service in finding my horse. You would do me an even greater one if you could now lay your hands on the murderer of John Straker."

"I have done so," said Holmes, quietly.

The Colonel and I stared at him in amazement. "You have got him! Where is he, then?" asked Ross, excitedly.

"He is here."

"Here! Where?"

"Right in front of me," answered my friend.

The Colonel flushed angrily. "I regard what you have just said as either a very bad joke or an insult," he said hotly.

Sherlock Holmes laughed. "I do not mean you, Colonel. The real murderer is standing immediately behind you!"

Holmes stepped past Ross and laid his hand upon the glossy neck of the thoroughbred horse.

"The horse!" cried both the Colonel and myself.

"Yes, the horse. And it may lessen his guilt if I add that it was done in self-defense. But there goes the bell. I stand to win a little on the next race. I'll explain everything later."

That evening Holmes, the Colonel, and I rode back to London by train. The journey was shortened by Holmes' fascinating explanation of what had occurred at the Dartmoor stable that Monday night.

"I confess," said Holmes, "that any theories I had formed by reading the papers were completely wrong. I went to the country believing that Simpson was the murderer, even though the evidence against him was not strong. It was while we were riding in the carriage to Straker's house that I remembered the stableboy had been served curried lamb. I saw then how important that fact was. I was marveling at how I could have overlooked such an important clue when we arrived at his house."

"I confess," said the Colonel, "that even now I cannot see how that fact helps us."

"It was the first link in my chain of reasoning.

Powdered opium is by no means tasteless. The flavor is not disagreeable, but it is noticeable. If it were mixed in an ordinary dish, the eater would taste it. A curry is full of spices and so would hide the taste completely. But this Fitzroy Simpson could not have arranged for the trainer's family to eat curry on that particular night. And it is too absurd to think that he came along with the powdered opium when they just happened to be eating curry. That is unthinkable. Therefore Simpson could not be our man. That left Straker and his wife. They were the only two people who could have chosen curried lamb for supper that night. The opium was added after the dish was set aside for the stableboy. This I knew because the others ate the same meal and yet were all right. Which of them, then, could get to the dish without the maid observing?

"Before deciding that question, I realized the importance of the silent dog. I knew there was a dog at the stable because the stableboy had threatened Simpson with it. Yet, someone had gone into the stable and unleashed the horse without the dog raising the alarm. The midnight visitor had to be someone the dog knew well.

"I was already convinced—or almost convinced—that it was John Straker. But why would he go down to the stable in the dead of night and take out Silver Blaze? For what purpose? For a dishonest one, obviously. Why else would he drug his own stableboy? At first I was at a loss as to why. I know of other cases where trainers have made great sums of money by betting on another horse and then making sure their own horse didn't run. Sometimes they prevent their horse from winning by getting the jockey to slow the horse down. But other times they have it done themselves. I hoped the contents of Straker's pockets might help me form a conclusion.

"And they did so. There was a very unusual knife in the dead man's hand. It was not the type of knife a man would choose for protection. Doctor Watson here explained what it was used for. He told us that it was used for the most delicate surgical operations. And that knife was to be used for a delicate operation. You must know, Colonel Ross, that it is possible to make a small cut on the tendons of a horse's leg. It can be done in such a way as to leave no trace at all. A horse nicked in such a way would develop a slight lameness. You would have thought it was due to a strain in exercise or a touch of rheumatism, but never foul play! With such a nick, the horse could not run."

"Villain! Scoundrel!" cried the Colonel.

"That is why John Straker wished to take the horse out on the moor. The horse would certainly react to the prick of the knife. His neighs could wake the sleepers in both the stable and the house. It was absolutely necessary to do it in the open air."

"I have been blind!" cried the Colonel. "Of course, that was why he needed the candle and the match."

"Undoubtedly. In examining his belongings, I even found the reason for the crime. As a man of the world, Colonel, you know that people don't carry other people's bills in their pockets. We all have enough trouble trying to pay our own. I at once concluded that Straker was leading a double life. The bill was from a dressmaker. This convinced me that a lady was mixed up in the case—and one with expensive tastes. You may pay your employees well, but they could not afford twenty-pound dresses for their

women! I then questioned Mrs. Straker as to the dress. It was clear by her answers that it had never reached her. I made a note of the dressmaker's address and borrowed a photograph of Straker.

"From that time on all was clear. Straker had led the horse to the hollow on the moor. From there his light could not be seen from the house. Simpson had dropped his scarf in his flight. Straker had picked it up for some reason. Perhaps to secure the horse's leg. Once in the hollow, he got behind the horse and struck a light. The horse was frightened by the sudden glare and he lashed out. His steel shoe struck Straker on the forehead. Straker had taken off his raincoat in order to do his delicate task. He held the surgical knife in his hand. As he fell, the knife gashed his thigh. Do I make myself clear?"

"Wonderful!" cried the Colonel. "Wonderful! You might have been there, Holmes!"

"My final shot was a very long one. It struck me that Straker would not attempt such a delicate operation without a little practice first. What could he practice on? My eyes fell upon the sheep. I asked the stableboy about them. His answer proved my guess was correct."

"You have made it perfectly clear, Mr. Holmes."

"When I returned to London I called on the dressmaker. She at once recognized the photograph of Straker. She said he was an excellent customer by the name of Darbyshire. He had a very dashing wife with a taste for expensive dresses. I have no doubt that this woman friend of his plunged him over his head and ears in debt. His debts then led him to this miserable plot!"

"You have explained all but one thing," cried the Colonel. "Where was the horse?"

"Ah, he bolted and was cared for by one of your neighbors. We must declare a truce on that particular subject, I think. There are certain things that even an unofficial detective must keep secret for the sake of the peace."

The Adventure of the Musgrave Ritual

The Adventure of the Musgrave Ritual is one of the few mysteries which supposedly took place before Watson and Holmes knew one another. It actually contains a number of mysteries: the mystery of the missing butler, the mystery of the missing maid, and then the main mystery of the Musgrave Ritual itself. There has been much discussion over the meaning of the Musgrave Ritual. However, Conan Doyle was fond of the tale and listed it as being one of his twelve best.

The Charles of the story is King Charles I of England. Civil war had broken out during his reign and in 1649 he was beheaded for treason. His son, also named Charles, eventually fled the country to France with his loyal followers. In 1660 he returned to his homeland. He put down the rebellion and restored order and the monarchy to England. In 1661 he was crowned Charles II, King of England.

The Adventure of
the Musgrave Ritual

Sherlock Holmes had one of the most organized and methodical of minds. But when it came to his personal habits, he was one of the most untidy men I have ever met! I myself am not the neatest of people, but with me there is a limit. Holmes kept his cigars in the coal-scuttle, his tobacco in the toe-end of a Persian slipper, and his unanswered letters attached by a jackknife to the very center of our wooden mantelpiece! I have also always believed that pistol practice is a distinctly outdoor sport. Holmes would sit in an armchair with his gun and cartridges and proceed to pump bullets into the opposite wall. I have to admit that I felt it neither enhanced the atmosphere nor the appearance of the room.

Our rooms were always full of chemicals. Souvenirs from past criminal cases were always turning up in the butter dish or some other odd place. But what truly bothered me were Holmes' papers. He hated to destroy documents, especially those connected to past cases. Yet he only managed to straighten them up once or twice a year. Month after month his papers would pile up. Eventually every corner of the room was stacked with them. And look out the man who tried to burn them or even store them away!

One winter's night we sat together by the fire. Holmes had just finished pasting clippings into his scrapbook. As usual, the room was scattered with paper. I suggested that he spend the next two hours making the room a bit more tidy. He could not deny that it needed straightening up. Without enthusiasm, Holmes went off to his bedroom. He came back, pulling a large tin box behind him. This he placed in the middle of the floor. He squatted down upon a stool in front of it and threw back the lid. I could see that it was a third full of bundles of paper. Each bundle was tied with red tape.

"My dear Watson," said Holmes mischievously, "if you knew what was in this box, you'd be asking me to pull papers out rather than put papers in."

"These must be the records of your early work," I said. "I have often wished that I had the notes of those cases."

"Yes, my boy. These were all done in my early days, before you had come along to write about me." He lifted bundle after bundle in a tender sort of way. "They are not all successes, Watson," said he. "But there are some rather interesting cases among them. Here's the record of the Tartleton murders, and the case of Vamberry, the wine merchant, and the adventure of the old Russian woman, and the curious affair of the aluminum crutch as well as a full account of the club-footed Ricoletti and his terrible wife. And here—ah, now! This is something really special!"

He dived down to the bottom of the chest and brought out a small wooden box with a sliding lid. From within he produced a crumpled piece of paper, an old-fashioned brass key, a peg of wood with a ball of string attached to it and three rusty old discs of metal.

"Well, my boy, what do you make of this lot?" Sherlock Holmes asked.

"It is a curious collection," I answered.

"Very curious. And the case in which they were involved will strike you even more curious."

"These relics have a history then?"

"So much so that they *are* history."

"What do you mean by that?"

Sherlock Holmes picked them up one by one and laid them along the edge of the table. Then he reseated himself in his chair and looked them over. There was a gleam of satisfaction in his eyes.

"These are all I have left to remind me of 'The Adventure of the Musgrave Ritual.' "

I had heard him mention the case more than once, but he had never told me the details.

"I would be very interested in hearing about the case."

"And I get to leave this litter right here!" Holmes cried, smiling. "Your desire for tidiness is short-lived, Watson! I should be glad to tell you of the Musgrave Ritual and have you write about it. There are many points in it which are quite unique in the criminal records of this country. A collection of my stories about my small achievements as a detective would certainly be incomplete without an account of this unusual adventure.

"You see me now when my name has become known far and wide. People travel to see me when the police cannot solve their doubtful cases. Even when you first met me I had already established myself as a consulting detective. You can hardly realize how difficult it was to start off in this unusual business of mine.

"When I first came to London I had rooms in Montague Street. They were just around the corner from the British Museum. I spent long hours at that museum studying everything I felt might help me in my work. Now and again fellow students would bring me a case to solve. The third of these cases was that of the Musgrave Ritual. It is to that one case that I owe my later success.

"Reginald Musgrave had studied at the same college as myself. We were slight acquaintances. He looked very aristocratic with his thin, high nose and large eyes. In fact, he was from one of the oldest families in the kingdom. His family had lived in Hurlstone Manor in Western Sussex. It is quite famous as an ancient estate. Once or twice we had a conversation at college. I can remember that he expressed a keen interest in my methods of observation and detection.

"For four years I had seen nothing of him. Then one morning he walked into my rooms in Montague Street. He had changed little. He was dressed like a man of fashion and seemed as distinguished as ever.

" 'How have things gone with you, Musgrave?' I asked after we had shaken hands.

" 'You probably heard of my poor father's death,' said he. 'He died about two years ago. Since then I have had the estate to manage and I am most busy. I understand, Holmes, that you are now using your amazing powers of observation professionally?'

" 'Yes,' said I, 'I have taken to living by my wits.'

" 'I am delighted to hear it. Your advice would be most valuable to me now. There are some very strange happenings down at Hurlstone. The police have not been able to shed any light upon the matter. It is really a most extraordinary business.'

"You can imagine, Watson, how eager I was to work on this case. I had been waiting for months for just such an opportunity. I was sure that I could succeed where others had failed."

" 'Pray let me have the details,' I cried.

"Reginald Musgrave sat down opposite me and lit the cigarette I pushed toward him.

" 'You know that I have to keep a large staff of servants at Hurlstone. It is a rambling old place and takes a good deal of looking after. Altogether there are eight maids, the cook, the butler, two footmen, and a boy. The garden and the stables, of course, have a separate staff.

" 'Of all the servants the butler, Brunton, has been in our service the longest. He had planned to be a schoolmaster, but had not been able to find work. My father hired him as our butler. He was a man of great energy and intelligence. He soon became invaluable in the household. He is a handsome man. He has been with us for twenty years but cannot be older than forty. With his looks and extraordinary talents—he can speak several languages and plays nearly every instrument—it is a bit surprising that he stayed on as a butler for so long. But I suppose he was comfortable and lacked the energy to make any change. The butler of Hurlstone is always remembered by those who visit us.

" 'But Brunton has one fault. He is a ladies' man. All the women are mad for him. When he was married it was all right. But his wife died. Since then he has been involved with one woman after the other. A few months ago we thought he was going to settle down again. He became engaged to Rachel Howells, our second housemaid. But he has broken up with her and now courts Janet Tregellis, the daughter of the head gamekeeper. Rachel is a very good girl, but she has a very excitable Welsh temperament. After he threw her over she became ill with fever. She has gone about the house like a madwoman ... or at least she did until yesterday. That was when the first drama occurred at Hurlstone.

" 'I have said that the house is a rambling one. One night last week—on Thursday night to be more exact—I could not sleep. And so at about two in the morning I rose from my bed. I lit a candle with the intention of reading a novel. The book I wanted to read, however, was in the billiard room. So I pulled on my dressing gown and started off to get it.

" 'To get to the billiard room I had to go down a flight of stairs and cross a hallway that led to the library and gunroom. I looked down this corridor and saw a light coming from the library. Naturally, my first thought was of burglars. The walls at Hurlstone are decorated with old weapons. I picked up a battle-axe. I left the candle behind me, tip-toed down the passage, and peeped in at the open door.

" 'Brunton, the butler, was in the library. He was sitting, fully-dressed, in an easy chair. He had a slip of paper upon his knee. It looked like a map. His forehead was sunk forward upon his hand in deep thought. I stood watching him in the darkness. I was dumb with astonishment. A small candle was on the edge of the table and shed a weak light. Suddenly he rose from his chair and walked over to a bureau. He unlocked it and pulled open one of its drawers. From this he took a piece of paper. He returned to his seat, flattened it out beside the candle and began to study it carefully. I was enraged at his calm inspection of my family documents. I took a step forward. It was then that Brunton saw me standing in the doorway. He sprang to his feet. His face was livid with fear. He quickly thrust the maplike paper into his pocket.

" ' "So!" said I, "this is how you repay us for the trust we have placed in you! You go through our private papers! You will leave my service tomorrow!"

" 'He looked like a man who is utterly crushed. He slunk past me without a word. The candle was still on the table. By its light I could see the piece of paper he had taken from the bureau. To my surprise, it was nothing of importance at all. It was simply a copy of the Musgrave Ritual. It is a curious old ceremony which each Musgrave recites on coming of age. The tradition has been carried on for centuries. It is of little interest to anyone except the family—and perhaps some archaeologist studying ancient family rituals.'

" 'We had better come back to that paper later,' said I.

" 'If you think it really necessary,' he answered. 'To continue my statement: I relocked the bureau with the key Brunton had left. Then I turned to go. I was surprised to find Brunton had returned and was standing before me.

" ' "Mr. Musgrave, sir," he cried. His voice was hoarse with emotion. "I can't bear disgrace, sir. I've always been proud. Disgrace would kill me. My blood will be on your head, sir—it will, indeed—if you drive me to despair. If you cannot keep me after what has passed, then for God's sake let me give you my resignation. I will leave in a month, as if of my own free will. I could stand that Mr. Musgrave. But I could not stand to be cast out in front of all the people I know so well."

" ' "You don't deserve much consideration, Brunton. Your conduct has been shocking. However you have been with the family a long time. I have no wish to bring public disgrace upon you. A month, however, is too long. Leave in one week, and tell people whatever you like."

" ' "Only a week, sir?" he cried in despair. "A fortnight, sir, two weeks . . ."

" ' "A week," I repeated.

" 'He crept away, his face sunk upon his breast like a broken man.

" 'For two days Brunton went about his duties as usual. I did not mention what had passed. I was curious to see how he was going to cover his disgrace. On the third morning, however, he did not appear after breakfast for his usual instructions. As I was leaving the dining room, I happened to meet Rachel Howells, the maid. She looked deathly pale.

" ' "You should be in bed," I said. "Come back to your duties when you are stronger."

" 'She looked at me with a strange expression.

" ' "I am strong enough, Mr. Musgrave," said she.

" ' "We will see what the doctor says," I answered. "You must stop work now. When you go downstairs tell Brunton I wish to see him."

" ' "The butler is gone, sir," said she.

" ' "Gone! Gone where?"

" ' "He is gone. No one has seen him. He is not in his room. Oh, yes, he is gone—he is gone!" She fell back against the wall with shriek after shriek of laughter. I was horrified at her mad behavior. I rushed to the bell to summon help. The girl was taken to her room, still screaming and sobbing. Meanwhile I made inquiries after Brunton. There was no doubt that he had disappeared. His bed had not been slept in. He had not been seen since he retired to his room the night before. Yet it was difficult to see how he left the house. Both the windows and doors were found locked in the morning as usual. His clothes, his watch, even his money, were found in his room. However, the black suit he usually wore was missing. His slippers, too, were gone, but his boots were left behind. Where, then, could butler Brunton have gone in the night and what could have become of him?

" 'We searched the house from cellar to garret. There was no trace of him. It was incredible to me that he could have gone away and left all his property behind. Yet where could he be? I called in the local police, but they found nothing. Rain had fallen the night before. We examined the lawn and the paths all around the house. Again we found nothing. It was then that a second drama occurred.

" 'For two days Rachel Howells had been ill. We had hired a nurse to sit with her day and night. On the third night after Brunton's disappearance Rachel was sleeping nicely. The nurse decided, therefore, to take a nap in the armchair. When she awoke in the early morning she found her patient gone. The window was open and there was no sign of Rachel. I was awakened immediately. The two footmen and I started off in search of the missing girl. We started our search directly under her window. We could see her footsteps in the earth. We followed them easily across the lawn. But they vanished at the edge of the lake, close by the gravel driveway which leads out of the grounds. The lake is eight feet deep. You can imagine our feelings when we saw that the girl's trail ended at its edge.

" 'Of course, we had the lake dragged at once. We did not find a trace of the girl. What we did bring up was a linen bag. It contained some rusty bits of metal and several dull-colored pieces of pebble or glass. This strange find was all that we could get from the lake. Despite all our efforts, we still know nothing of the fate of Rachel Howells or Richard Brunton. The country police are at their wits end. And so, I have come to you.'

"I listened eagerly to this extraordinary tale. I tried in my mind to find a common thread which would pull these strange events together.

"The facts of the case were these: The butler was gone and the maid was gone. The maid had loved the butler, but had afterward reason to hate him. She was of Welsh blood and so was fiery and passionate. She had been terribly excited after his disappearance. She had flung a bag into the lake. That bag had contained some curious objects. All these facts were important. Yet none gave me a clue into the true heart of the matter. What was the starting point of this chain of events? There lay the end of this tangled thread.

" 'I must see that paper, Musgrave,' said I. 'The one Brunton took from the bureau.'

" 'This Ritual of ours is an absurd business,' he answered. 'But it is very ancient. I have a copy of the questions and answers here.'

"He handed me the very paper which I have here, Watson. This is the strange Ritual each Musgrave had to recite when he reached manhood. I will read you the questions and answers:

" 'WHOSE WAS IT?'
" 'HIS WHO IS GONE.'
" 'WHO SHALL HAVE IT?'
" 'HE WHO WILL COME.'
" 'WHERE WAS THE SUN?'
" 'OVER THE OAK.'
" 'WHERE WAS THE SHADOW?'

" 'UNDER THE ELM.'
" 'HOW WAS IT STEPPED?'
" 'NORTH BY TEN AND BY TEN,
    EAST BY FIVE AND BY FIVE,
    SOUTH BY TWO AND BY TWO,
    WEST BY ONE AND BY ONE,
    AND SO UNDER.'
" 'WHAT SHALL WE GIVE FOR IT?'
" 'ALL THAT IS OURS.'
" 'WHY SHOULD WE GIVE IT?'
" 'FOR THE SAKE OF THE TRUST.'

" 'The original has no date. But the spelling is of the seventeenth century,' remarked Musgrave. 'I am afraid it can be of little help to you in solving this mystery.'

" 'What it does,' said I, 'is give us another mystery—one which is even more interesting than the first. It may be that the solution to one may prove to be the solution to the other. You will excuse me, Musgrave, if I say that your butler appears to have been a very clever man. He seems to have understood the meaning of this Ritual more than ten generations of his masters.'

" 'I hardly follow you,' said Musgrave. 'The paper seems to me to be of no practical importance.'

" 'But to me it seems immensely practical. I fancy Brunton saw it the same way. He had probably seen this Ritual before the night you caught him.'

" 'It is very possible. We did not hide it.'

" 'I imagine that he simply wanted to refresh his memory that last time. You say he had some sort of map as well? And that he thrust it in his pocket on seeing you?'

" 'That is true. But what could Brunton have to do with this old family custom of ours? And what does this rigamarole mean?'

" 'I don't think we'll have much difficulty finding that out,' I said. 'With your permission, we will take the first train down to Sussex. We can go more deeply into the matter there.'

"That afternoon we went down to Hurlstone Manor. Perhaps you have seen pictures and read descriptions of that famous old building. It is built in the shape of an 'L.' The long arm is the more modern portion while the short arm is the ancient part of the building. The date 1607 is chiseled over the door in the center of the original wing. Experts say that the beams and stonework are even older than this. Its enormously thick walls and tiny windows forced the family to build a newer, more modern building. The old one is now used as a storehouse and a cellar. A splendid park with fine old trees surrounds the house. The lake lies close by the drive and is about two hundred yards from the building.

"I was convinced that there were not three separate mysteries here. There was but one. I felt that if I could only read the Musgrave Ritual correctly, I could solve its mystery—and find the missing butler and maid. I now turned all my energies to that task. I asked myself why the butler wanted to understand this old Ritual. The answer was plain: Because he saw something in it—something which generations of country squires had not understood. He must have expected to gain something by figuring out its questions and answers. What, then, did the Ritual mean? And what did it have to do with the butler and the maid's strange disappearance?

"It seemed obvious to me that the measurements were directions to some particular spot on the property. We now had to find that spot. There were two clues or guides—one was the oak and the other was the elm. As to the oak, there could be no question at all. Right in front of the house there stood a great giant oak. It was one of the most magnificent trees I have ever seen.

" 'Was that tree there when your Ritual was first drawn up?' said I as we drove past.

" 'It was probably there a thousand years ago. It has a girth of 23 feet!'

" 'Have you any old elms?' I asked.

" 'There used to be a very old one over yonder. It was struck by lightning ten years ago. We cut down the stump.'

" 'Can you still see where it used to be?' I asked.

" 'Oh, yes.'

" 'There are no other elms?'

" 'No old ones, but plenty of beeches,' said Musgrave.

" 'I should like to see where it grew,' I said.

"We got out of the carriage and he led me to where the elm had stood. It was nearly midway between the oak and the house. My investigation seemed to be progressing.

" 'I suppose it is impossible to find out how high the elm was?' I asked.

" 'I can tell you that at once. It was 64 feet,' answered Musgrave. 'When I was a lad my tutor made me measure the heights of things. I had to work out the height of every tree and building on the estate.'

"This was an unexpected piece of luck. My information was coming more quickly than I could have hoped for!

" 'Tell me,' I asked, 'did your butler ever ask you that question?'

"Reginald Musgrave looked at me in astonishment. 'Now that you call it to mind, Brunton *did* ask me about the height of the tree some months ago. He said he needed to know it to settle an argument with the grooms.'

"This was excellent news, Watson. It showed me that I was on the right road. The ritual had said: 'Where was the sun?' 'Over the oak.' I looked up at the sun. It was low in the heavens. I calculated that in less than one hour it would lie just above the topmost branches of the old oak. One instruction in the old Ritual would then be met. 'Where was the shadow?' it had asked. 'Under the elm.' I now had to find out where the end of the elm's shadow would fall when the sun was just above the oak."

"But that must have been difficult, Holmes. The elm was no longer there!"

"If Brunton could do it, then so could I. I went with Musgrave to his study and whittled myself a peg. I attached a very long string to it. I marked off each yard with a knot. Next I fetched Musgrave's six-foot fishing rod. Musgrave and I went back to where the elm had stood. I looked up. The sun was just over the oak. I stuck the rod into the earth. Its shadow pointed toward the the house and measured nine feet in length. What had I learned by this? At this time of day a six-foot rod casts a nine foot shadow—the shadow was half-again the rod's length. Therefore, a 64-foot tree would cast a shadow 96 feet long at the same time of day. Likewise, the tree's shadow would point in the same direction as had the rod's. I placed my string at the base of the rod. This was my starting point. I then began to walk in the direction of its shadow. As I walked I measured the distance with my string. Ninety-six feet later I found myself almost at the wall of the manor. I

thrust my peg into the spot. Then I saw a small hole in the ground only two inches away. You can imagine my delight, Watson. I knew that it had been made by Brunton. I was still on the right trail.

"The Ritual had next said to 'step north ten and by ten, east five and by five, south two and by two and west one and by one.' Ten steps north with each foot took me alongside the wall. Again I marked the spot. Then I carefully paced off five double steps to the east and two double steps to the south. They brought me to the old door. And 'west one and by one' seemed to mean that I was to go two paces beyond that door. I should now be standing where the secret of the Musgrave Ritual was hidden.

"The sun shone down on the old gray stones. They were firmly cemented and had not been moved in years. I tapped upon the floor, but it sounded the same all over. There was no sign of a crack or crevice. Never had I been so disappointed. Luckily, Musgrave had begun to understand what I was doing. He was now as excited as myself. He took out the Ritual to check its instructions.

" 'And under!' he cried. 'You have forgotten the "and so under." '

"I had thought 'and so under' meant that we were to dig. But now I saw that I was wrong. 'Is there a cellar under us?' I cried.

" 'Yes, and it is as old as the house. Down here, through this door!'

"We went down a winding stone staircase. My companion struck a match. A lantern stood nearby on a barrel. He lit it and the cellar brightened. There was no doubt that we had come to the right place . . . and that others had been there recently.

"The cellar had been used to store planks of wood. Someone had pulled the planks to one side. In the center of the floor was one particularly large flagstone. A rusted iron ring was attached to it. To this was tied a woolen muffler.

" 'By Jove!' cried Musgrave, 'that's Brunton's muffler! I have seen it on him. I could swear it! What has he been doing here?'

"I suggested that we call the local police immediately. It was not long before two strong policemen arrived on the scene. I then tried to raise up the stone by pulling on the muffler. I could barely move it. One of the policemen came to my aid. Together, we managed to slide the stone to one side. A black hole loomed beneath. We all peered into the pit. Musgrave knelt at its edge and pushed the lantern down into it.

"A small chamber about seven feet deep and four feet square lay open beneath us. To one side was a squat wooden box. Its hinge lid lay open and an old-fashioned key was in its lock. The box was covered in a thick layer of dust. Damp and worms had eaten through the wood. Mold was growing within. Several discs of metal were scattered over the bottom of the box. They seemed to be old coins of some sort. The box contained nothing else.

"At that moment, however, we had little thought for that old chest. Our eyes were glued to what lay beside it. There, frozen in position, crouched the figure of a man. He was dressed in a suit of black and his arms were outstretched toward us. All the blood had drained from his face and it was now unrecognizable. But the height, the dress, and the hair convinced Musgrave that this was his missing butler. He had been dead for some days. There was

no wound or bruise on his body to show how he had met
his death. The police dragged the body from its tomb and
carried it away.

"I must confess that I was disappointed with my
investigation at this point. I had thought the discovery of
the hiding-place would reveal both what was the Ritual's
secret and what had happened to the butler and the maid.
But now it seemed only to have raised further questions.
What had been in the chest? Why had the Musgrave's
hidden it so securely and put the directions to its
whereabouts into such a curious Ritual? And the butler . . .
how had he met his fate? And the maid . . . what part had
she played in this drama? I sat myself down upon a barrel
and thought out the entire matter most carefully.

"You know my methods in such cases, Watson. I put
myself in the butler's place. He had discovered the Ritual
and had figured out that it contained a message to future
Musgraves. The message was that they had been entrusted
with some object of importance. It was to be found
according to the directions in the Ritual. He knew that
something of value was to be found at the trail's end. And
so he worked out the instructions and came upon the huge
stone in the floor. But it was too heavy for him to move
alone. He needed someone's aid. But whose? The windows
and the doors of the manor were barred every night. It
would be risky to let someone in and out. There was too
much chance of being discovered. No, far better to use
someone who lived right in the house. Of course, he would
think of Rachel Howells, the maid. She had loved him. He
had thrown her over for someone else. But he probably
thought he could win her back with flattery. And so it
seemed that he had.

"Together they went down to the cellar. But it must have been difficult to raise that heavy stone. A large Sussex policeman and I had trouble enough doing it. They needed something to help them in their great task. But what would they use? I tried to think what I would have done. I walked over to the nearest pile of wood. It was not long before I found what I was looking for. One particular plank of wood had a large gash or groove at one end. They had managed to lift up the stone slightly. They had then slipped this plank into the crack and used it as a lever to help them shift the stone to one side.

"Only one person could fit into the small hole. That person was Brunton. He had crawled down, while the girl had waited above. Brunton had unlocked the box and handed up the contents to Rachel. And then—what had happened? Had the plank slipped and the stone snapped shut by chance? Or did the maid suddenly want revenge for the butler's faithlessness? Had she knocked away the wooden support and sent the stone slab crashing back into place? Brunton must have screamed and scratched at the stone in terror. In my mind, I could see Rachel as she clutched at her treasure and rushed up the winding stairs. Her ex-lover's cries must have rung in her ears as she fled.

"This then was the cause of her white face, her shaken nerves, her hysterical laughter. But what had been in the box . . . and what had she done with it? It had to have been the old metal and pebbles dragged from the lake. She had thrown them in the water to remove the last trace of her terrible crime.

"For twenty minutes I sat motionless thinking the matter out. Musgrave still peered down into the hole, his face deathly pale.

" 'These must be the coins of King Charles I,' he said. 'He was the King of England when the Ritual was written.'

" 'And we may find something else of Charles I,' I cried suddenly. 'Let me see the contents of the bag you fished from the lake.'

"We went up to his study and he lay its contents before me. The metal was almost black and the stones were dark and dull. I rubbed one of them on my sleeve. It sparkled brilliantly. The metal work was in the shape of a double ring, but it had been bent and twisted out of its original shape.

" 'If my mind serves me, Charles I was executed. His son, Charles II fled the country with many of the royal families. They probably had to leave their most precious possessions buried behind them. I am sure they intended to return for them in more peaceful times.'

" 'My ancestor, Sir Ralph Musgrave, was a knight during King Charles' day. He later left England with Charles II,' said my friend.

" 'Ah, indeed!' I answered. 'Well, I think we now have the last link in this mystery. It is sad that you had to make such a discovery through so tragic a drama. But you now possess a relic of truly great historic value.'

" 'What is it, then?' Musgrave gasped in astonishment.

" 'It is nothing less than the ancient crown of the Kings of England,' Sherlock Holmes answered.

" 'The crown!' Musgrave exclaimed.

" 'Precisely. Consider what the Ritual says. How does it run? "Whose was it?" "His who is gone." It had belonged to Charles I, but Charles I was now dead. Then, "Who shall have it?" "He who will come." That was Charles II. He had fled the country, but would later return to be king. There can be no doubt that this battered and shapeless object once crowned royal heads.'

" 'And how did it get into the pond?' Musgrave asked.

" 'That is a question which will take some time to answer,' I said and began to explain my theory.

" 'And why didn't Charles II recover his crown when he returned to England?' asked Musgrave.

" 'Ah, that we may never know. It is likely that only one Musgrave knew where the crown was buried. He probably died while Charles II was abroad. By some oversight he must have left this Ritual without explaining its meaning. From that day to this it has been handed down from father to son . . . until it fell into the hands of a man who solved its mystery and lost his life for it.

"And that's the story of the Musgrave Ritual, Watson. They now have the crown down at Hurlstone. I am sure they will show it to you if you mention my name. Nothing was ever heard of Rachel Howells. She probably carried herself—and the memory of her crime—to some distant land."

With that, Sherlock Holmes shut his tin box and dragged it back into his bedroom. The bundles of paper scattered all about remained exactly as they were. As for me, I forgot all about the mess, and happily spent the rest of the evening writing down "The Adventure of the Musgrave Ritual."

BOOK ONE

Sir Arthur Conan Doyle's
THE ADVENTURES OF
SHERLOCK HOLMES

Adapted for young readers by Catherine Edwards Sadler

Whose footsteps are those on the stairs of 221-B Baker Street, home of Mr. Sherlock Holmes, the world's greatest detective? And what incredible mysteries will challenge the wits of the genius sleuth this time?

A Study In Scarlet In the first Sherlock Holmes story ever written, Holmes and Watson embark on their first case together—an intriguing murder mystery.
The Red-headed League Holmes comes to the rescue in a most unusual heist!
The Man With The Twisted Lip Is this a case of murder, kidnapping, or something totally unexpected?

Join the uncanny and extraordinary Sherlock Holmes, and his friend and chronicler, Dr. Watson as they tackle dangerous crimes and untangle the most intricate mysteries.

AVON **C** CAMELOT

AN AVON CAMELOT ORIGINAL ● $2.50/$3.25
(ISBN: 0-380-78089-5)

BOOK TWO

Sir Arthur Conan Doyle's
THE ADVENTURES OF
SHERLOCK HOLMES

Adapted for young readers by Catherine Edwards Sadler

The Sign of the Four What starts as a case about a missing person, becomes one of poisonous murder, deceit, and deep intrigue leading to a remote island off the coast of India.

The Adventure of the Blue Carbuncle It's up to Holmes to find the crook when the Countess' diamond is stolen.

The Adventure of the Speckled Band Can Holmes save a young woman from a mysterious death, or will he be too late?

Join the uncanny and extraordinary Sherlock Holmes, and his friend and chronicler, Dr. Watson, as they tackle dangerous crimes and untangle the most intricate mysteries.

AVON CAMELOT

**AN AVON CAMELOT ORIGINAL • $2.50/$3.25
(ISBN: 0-380-78097-6)**

BOOK FOUR

Sir Arthur Conan Doyle's

THE ADVENTURES OF
SHERLOCK HOLMES

Adapted for young readers by Catherine Edwards Sadler

The Adventure of the Reigate Puzzle Holmes comes near death to unravel a devilish case of murder and blackmail.

The Adventure of the Crooked Man The key to this strange mystery lies in the deadly secrets of a wicked man's past.

The Adventure of the Greek Interpreter Sherlock's brilliant older brother joins Holmes on the hunt for a bunch of ruthless villains in a case of kidnapping.

The Adventure of the Naval Treaty Only Holmes can untangle a case that threatens the national security of England, and becomes a matter of life and death.

Join the uncanny and extraordinary Sherlock Holmes, and his friend and chronicler Dr. Watson, as they tackle dangerous crimes and untangle the most intricate mysteries.

AVON CAMELOT

AN AVON CAMELOT ORIGINAL • $2.50/$3.25
(ISBN: 0-380-78113-1)

Avon Camelot Books are available at your bookstore. Or, you may use Avon's special mail order service. Please state the title and code number and send with your check or money order for the full price, plus $1.00 per copy to cover postage and handling, to: AVON BOOKS, Dept BP, Box 767, Rt. 2, Dresden, TN 38225

Please allow 6-8 weeks for delivery.